"You can't go on keeping me here!"

Lisa's voice was shaking. "It just isn't right!"

"Right?" Yusuf's hand still held her chin. "By what right, *mademoiselle,* did you invade my privacy with your silly warnings?"

Lisa's pride prevented her from begging. "You're an arrogant selfish monster and I wish I'd never come on board your wretched yacht!"

His mouth tightened in a straight line as he pulled her close to his lean hard body. "So do I," he murmured. *"Mon dieu,* so do I."

Seconds later the warm thrilling touch of his mouth parted her lips, bruising in its hardness. Alarming and exciting and breathtaking in its fierceness.

When he let her go Lisa looked up at him with stunned eyes. Never before had she been so affected by a single kiss....

Other titles by

REBECCA STRATTON IN HARLEQUIN ROMANCES

1942—THE FIRE AND THE FURY
1955—MOON TIDE
1976—THE GODDESS OF MAVISU
1991—ISLE OF THE GOLDEN DRUM
2006—PROUD STRANGER
2018—CHATEAU D'ARMOR
2036—THE ROAD TO GAFSA
2050—GEMINI CHILD
2078—GIRL IN A WHITE HAT
2091—INHERIT THE SUN
2106—MORE THAN A DREAM
2131—SIGN OF THE RAM
2141—THE VELVET GLOVE
2154—DREAM OF WINTER
2173—SPINDRIFT
2180—IMAGE OF LOVE
2201—BARGAIN FOR PARADISE
2222—THE CORSICAN BANDIT
2261—LOST HERITAGE
2268—THE EAGLE OF THE VINCELLA
2274—LARK IN AN ALIEN SKY

Other titles by

REBECCA STRATTON IN HARLEQUIN PRESENTS

106—YELLOW MOODS
121—THE WARM WIND OF FARIK

by

REBECCA STRATTON

Harlequin Books

TORONTO • LONDON • NEW YORK • AMSTERDAM
SYDNEY • HAMBURG • PARIS • STOCKHOLM

Original hardcover edition published in 1979
by Mills & Boon Limited

ISBN 0-373-02303-0

Harlequin edition published December 1979

Printed in U.S.A.

CHAPTER ONE

LISA had doubts. She had any number of doubts, but mostly she doubted the wisdom of Geoffrey getting himself so closely involved in the latest activity the group had planned. So far their activities had been fairly innocuous; merely the handing out of leaflets, printed at their own expense, and proclaiming their feelings about various matters which they considered were unjust.

In this instance, however, it had been decided to go beyond the passive handing out of leaflets, and make some more noticeable form of protest. Lisa's own feelings were mixed at the moment, for she felt both apprehension and excitement, but she was very glad to have Geoffrey with her because he was guaranteed to inspire confidence.

Geoffrey Mason was good-looking, earnest and very English. Even in the heat of the Moroccan summer he was wearing a formal suit with a collar and tie, instead of slacks and an open-necked shirt which would have been much more comfortable. And it wasn't as if he was going to be seen in the same way that she was herself.

To Lisa, Geoffrey always looked exactly what he was, and she saw it as by no means a derogatory opinion. A junior official with the Diplomatic Service, he was a diplomat in the making, and destined to follow in the esteemed footsteps of his father. But the Diplomatic Service was unlikely to look kindly upon a junior member of its staff who embroiled himself in the activities of a group like *Balek*! so that she wondered if he fully realised what a serious effect his involvement could have on a very promising career.

She would hate anything to happen to him, for she was really quite fond of him, though her attachment was in no way romantic at the moment, and there was a hint of regret mingled with the other emotions she felt, when she looked at him. He took everything so seriously that sometimes the others found him amusing, though Lisa never did.

'You're very quiet,' she told him, watching the street lights flick little dark shadows across his face. 'Are you very nervous?'

Geoffrey half-turned his head for a moment, and his sober grey eyes warmed with pleasure when he looked at her. Most men found Lisa pleasing to look at, no matter how sober and serious they might be, and Geoffrey was no exception. Endowed with something more than just beauty, she had a freshness and charm and an awareness of people that made them warm to her immediately; and a sexual awareness of men that attracted them to her without any special effort on her part.

'I keep realising how much could go wrong once you get in there,' Geoffrey admitted cautiously, and Lisa could not restrain a faint smile at his caution, because it was so typical of Geoffrey to see drawbacks where there need not be any. 'We didn't give enough time to planning this, Lisa. It could go awfully wrong.'

Lisa pulled a face. She knew just how wrong it could go, but she did not want to think about it. 'What choice had we?' she asked. 'We tried every other means of contacting him and it was useless. But you really shouldn't have come, Geoffrey, you're risking so much.'

'Possibly.'

Lisa knew very well that his apparent carelessness was assumed, for Geoffrey was never offhand about anything, and definitely not about anything that could affect his career, so he must have their present cause very much at heart. 'You could back out,' she suggested, but knew full well he never would once he was committed. 'I wouldn't blame you, Geoffrey, and I could carry this out on my own.'

'You certainly will not!' Geoffrey declared firmly. 'And you'll find you need someone close by, no matter how confident you feel at the moment. Just the same, I feel badly about doing nothing more constructive than skulk about outside while you take all the risks.'

'Oh, what nonsense!' She gave him a smile that sought to make up for the impression she had given. 'And I certainly didn't mean to sound as if I didn't need you; I do.'

He said nothing more for the moment, but Lisa knew it would take a great deal to convince him that he should keep a low profile in the present situation. It was all too likely to blow up into something that could hit the local headlines, and she became less easy about her own part, the nearer they got to their destination. The man they had to deal with had power and influence, and she had few illusions about his possible reaction.

This was something much different from sitting in the little café where the group habitually met, sipping mint tea and nibbling sticky sweet pastries. This was likely to go well beyond the effect of leaflets handed out to an only mildly interested public, and she was unable to decide at the moment whether she felt more fearful or excited about her own part in it.

She knew quite a few Moroccans, there were even one or two in the group, but she had lived in Casablanca for only a little over a year. Having lived with an aunt for several years, she had suddenly made up her mind to come out and join her father, who was an industrial adviser with the Moroccan government, and her introduction to the group had come about almost by accident. A girl friend had taken her along to one of their gatherings, when she expressed her curiosity.

Lisa would probably not have troubled herself about them after that first time, but Geoffrey Mason had been there that evening and they had taken an immediate liking to one another. Certainly she had never visualised the likelihood of her being elected to the role of liaison between the group and the object of their present indignation.

'Lisa, you're quite sure you *want* to do this, aren't you?'

Geoffrey's voice broke into her thoughts and she smiled at him almost automatically. 'Yes, of course I'm sure,' she said, and was not quite sure whether or not he noticed her slight grimace when she said it. 'Anyway, the moment is at hand now, as they say, and I can't get cold feet at the last minute.'

'You could,' Geoffrey insisted quite seriously. 'I wouldn't blame you.'

Lisa laughed, though it was a short sharp sound that grated harshly on her own sensitive ears. 'But the rest of them would, and anyway, I'd feel as if I'd let everyone down very badly if I backed out now.' She glanced out of the car window at the brightly-lit, modern streets of Casablanca and leaned back in her seat, folding her hands on her lap. 'It might even be exciting,' she told him, then glanced at his shadowed and serious face that looked somehow older in the harshness of street lighting. 'Will I pass as a guest at one of Sheik Abahn's grand parties, do you think?'

Nothing loath to take another look, Geoffrey turned his head for as long as he safely could. Her light brown hair was streaked with sun-bleached blonde and grew to well below her shoulders, framing a small oval face, with a full soft mouth and brown-fringed blue eyes, which even though she smiled showed something of the nervousness she felt but refused to succumb to.

The dress he was being asked to pass judgment on

clung lovingly to her body as far as the waist, leaving the rest of her slender shape shrouded in clouds of pale yellow silk. A wispy scarf of the same material covered her head and kept the breeze through the open window from making too much disorder of her hair, and she had it slightly raised at chin level so that it gave the appearance of a half-veil and hinted at the East, despite her very European colouring.

'You look beautiful,' Geoffrey said, serious as always. 'Much too lovely to go in there alone and tackle Yusuf ben Dacra.'

'Well, maybe it will help me convince him.'

She rewarded him with a smile, but her heart was hammering urgently again when she considered the mission she had been entrusted with. Yusuf ben Dacra was the adopted son of Sheik Abahn el Boudri, one of Morocco's most successful and influential men, and it was his scheme for the demolition of a native village to make way for a luxury hotel that was the subject of the group's objection. Her main doubt was if such a man as Yusuf ben Dacra sounded to be would even deign to listen to her, even if she was able to get near him.

From the corner of her eye she was aware of Geoffrey looking at her again briefly, she suspected he was still unconvinced of her ability to tackle their quarry alone. 'I'm not happy about this, Lisa,' he said, confirming her suspicion. 'I really think I should come in with you.'

'Oh no, we can't change the plan now, I'll be perfectly all right.' She hastily subdued her own misgivings and shook her head. 'I stand more chance of getting in on my own via the street door and the garden as we planned. Then all I have to do is tell Yusuf ben Dacra that unless he abandons his scheme for destroying Zobi the group—we—will take strong action to make sure that he does.'

'Put like that it's a definite threat,' Geoffrey said, as if it had never occurred to him before that that was exactly what it was, and Lisa gave him a brief curious frown.

'Well, it *is* a threat, isn't it?' she asked.

'Yes. Yes, of course. But you seem so cool,' he observed, almost as if he resented the fact. 'Aren't you at all nervous?'

Lisa smiled and wrinkled her nose, as reluctant to admit it as he had been. 'I have a funny feeling in my stomach,' she confessed, 'but that could just as easily be excitement. To be honest I'm not quite sure what I feel like at the moment. But whatever it is, I shall be better for knowing you're waiting for me when I eventually come out. I have to make myself known to deliver our ultimatum, and after that I'll almost certainly get thrown out, so it'll be quite a comfort to know you're hovering in the wings with a car to take me home.'

'That's if he doesn't have you arrested.'

Lisa's heart gave a great lurch of panic and she turned her head and stared at him for a moment. It had always been on the cards, she supposed, but she had not been faced with it as a definite possibility until now. If Yusuf ben Dacra was as ruthless and callous as his scheme for Zobi suggested he was, then he was unlikely to think twice about having her arrested for threatening him, and he and his family were a force to be reckoned with in Casablanca.

In the circumstances it was not easy to do, but she took her wavering courage firmly in hand and laughed with a lightness she was far from feeling. 'If I'm arrested, then you'll have to come and bail me out,' she said. 'But I hope it won't come to that.'

'So do I,' Geoffrey told her with a good deal less optimism. 'But he's something of a hard case, I imagine, and he might decide you've overstepped the mark by making a threat against his latest project.'

Had it been anyone else, Lisa might have suspected he was joking, but not Geoffrey; he never joked, and especially about anything as embarrassing as being arrested on the premises of an important man like Sheik Abahn.

'*Would* he?' she asked, after a few seconds of silence during which she tried to still the cowardly small voice that offered a way out. And Geoffrey reached out to clasp one of her hands briefly in his cool slim fingers.

'Surprise is the element here,' he told her. 'If you can deliver the ultimatum and get out as quickly as possible, I don't see him making too much of a fuss with a house full of guests.'

'I hope not.' Lisa felt suddenly much more involved, and at the same time she realised just how little she knew about the man she was to tackle on his own home ground. In the circumstances, she felt, it might be an advantage to find out a little more about him rather than dwell on what was likely to happen when she met him face to face. 'How much *do* we know about Yusuf ben Dacra?' she asked. 'I might as well know what—or who—I'm up against.'

Geoffrey took a moment to consider. 'Not really very much,' he confessed after a moment or two. 'We know that he's Sheik Abahn's adopted son, whatever that implies.'

Lisa glanced at him curiously. 'Does that mean you think he might *be* the sheik's son? Literally, I mean?'

Geoffrey shrugged, as if the question made him uneasy. He was already diplomat enough to hesitate about committing himself firmly on a matter as delicate as whether or not a man as important as Sheik Abahn el Boudri kept an illegitimate son under his roof.

'It has been suggested,' he allowed cautiously, 'but as far as I know it's nothing more than rumour and I shouldn't have repeated it. There are also rumours that he isn't entirely Arab, but has some European blood; but that I'm inclined to doubt, from his looks.'

Lisa gave him a swift, enquiring look. 'You've seen him in the flesh?'

'Just once,' said Geoffrey. 'I attended a meeting with one of our senior staff members, and he was there. He speaks almost perfect English, impeccable French, some Spanish and quite a bit of Italian, as well as his native Arabic, of course.'

Lisa allowed for the man's linguistic skill, but she was more interested in his physical aspect. 'But what does he actually *look* like?' she asked.

Geoffrey shrugged, as offhand about another man's looks as most of his sex. 'Like a Moroccan. Very dark, quietly spoken, maybe a little taller than most. He's also a brilliant civil engineer, and an excellent businessman with a reputation for straight dealing.'

'And yet he's proposing to do that to some of his own people?' Lisa frowned. 'More than likely his reputation for straight dealing was thought up by a good publicity man, Geoffrey. No straight-dealing man would do what he's proposing to do at Zobi.'

'Maybe you're right,' Geoffrey allowed, but was obviously far more concerned about her going in alone to see the man they were discussing, than about the character of the man himself. 'Whatever he's like,' he said, 'I don't like you going in there on your own, Lisa. The more I think about it the less I like it, and I insist on coming in with you.'

'And I insist on going in alone,' Lisa told him with such firmness that he looked at her in surprise. Seeing his expression, Lisa placed a hand on his arm as he turned the car down one of the smaller side streets through the older part of the town. 'I'll be perfectly all right, Geoffrey, so let's not argue about it any more, please.'

He did not answer, but his reluctance was obvious and he looked even more than usually serious when he stopped the car about half way along a small quiet street that seemed little more than a corridor between high walls. Behind those walls were scented gardens and patios and the fine houses of wealthy Moroccans like Sheik Abahn, and Lisa could just catch the whispering shush of trees somewhere when the engine stopped and her ears became attuned to the ensuing quiet.

Half-turning in her seat, she shivered as the same misgivings came crowding back once more. Contemplating the dimly-lit street between the high walls she was struck by the fact that it looked alarmingly like a prison, and in view of Geoffrey's remarks earlier, it was hardly a comforting thought.

At intervals along the walls small doors were let into the stonework and, unless their informant had misled them, the one giving access to the grounds of Sheik Abahn's house should be unlocked. 'This is it,' said Geoffrey, and Lisa noticed that even out here in the empty street he spoke in a whisper.

He had stopped the car directly opposite one of the doors and Lisa sat for a moment staring at it. Solid and thick and strengthened with iron braces, it was designed to keep out unwelcome callers, and Lisa was only too conscious of the fact that in this case that meant her. It was not a fact guaranteed to inspire confidence.

'Are you positive it will be unlocked?' she asked, and Geoffrey nodded.

'That's our information—it's never kept locked, apparently. Sheik Abahn must be a very trusting man.'

'Oh, Geoffrey, don't make it worse!' she begged, and turned reproachful eyes on him. 'I hate to think I'm taking advantage of a man's trusting nature.'

'Well, maybe he's just careless,' Geoffrey suggested,

but it was clear his mind was on other things. 'Lisa, I think I should——'

'Oh well, it's now or never,' Lisa interrupted swiftly, and turned to smile at him before opening the car door. 'I'm the elected spokesman, and I'll get to Yusuf ben Dacra or die in the attempt.'

Treating the words seriously, although they were made in jest, Geoffrey attempted to put a detaining hand on her arm as she opened the door. 'I wish you wouldn't say things like that—it isn't funny, Lisa.'

She was out of the car and standing on the footpath before he had time to leave his seat, and she stood for a moment looking both ways along that narrow street. There was no one else about and the place seemed to have a distinctly sinister air that brought little shivers to her spine for a moment before she recovered her nerve. She was glad when Geoffrey came and stood beside her, even though it was for only a few minutes.

Her heart was thudding and the palms of her hands, when she rolled her fingers into them, felt moist and clammy. Lisa did not remember ever having felt fear before, but she felt it then while she stood in the shadow of Sheik Abahn's walls and tried to find courage to open a small door. For a moment she almost succumbed to temptation and agreed to let Geoffrey come in with her, but then she remembered how serious it would be for him if Yusuf ben Dacra did call in the police and have them arrested.

'I'll see how right we are,' she whispered, taking herself firmly in hand, and left Geoffrey standing in the middle of the pavement, looking left and right, up and down the street. Her legs trembled alarmingly as she approached the door and she was horribly uncertain whether or not she wanted their informant to be right about it being left open.

Grasping the handle firmly, she pushed, and the door

gave so easily that she had to quickly pull it towards her again, leaving it no more than an inch or so ajar. She was breathing lightly and noisily, as if it was an effort to draw breath at all, and just for a moment she wondered what on earth she was going to do if there was someone immediately the other side when she went through. It was not something they had taken into account, and she wondered how many more possible snags she would discover before the evening was through.

Turning to speak to Geoffrey, she tried to make her voice sound light and faintly triumphant. 'I'm in!' she whispered.

She heard Geoffrey's voice behind her as she pushed the door wider, but his words were lost in the thudding hammer-beat of her heart. She had expected to see gardens immediately beyond the door, but instead, when she put a cautious head round the edge, she saw a tunnel-like passage that at first looked even more grim than the street outside, and was claustrophobic in its narrowness.

Alarmed by the unexpected, she hesitated about going in, and she sensed Geoffrey's watching eyes as he stood in the deserted street behind her. 'Lisa?'

His whispered query roused her, and she used one hand to signal him to silence, then stepped inside. 'It's all right,' she told him, over her shoulder. 'I'm just getting my bearings, that's all.'

It was dark and it smelled damp and cold, but she could see a glimpse of light at the far end and just catch the vague, indeterminate sound of voices, unrecognisable at first, but then strangely reassuring. Making up her mind, she turned and gave Geoffrey a brief wave, then closed the door carefully behind her.

Her hands were unsteady as she gathered her skirts about her to keep them from brushing on the walls, and she made her way slowly along the narrow passage, keeping her eyes all the time on the promise of light at the other end. She emerged rather sooner than she expected, and coming suddenly into the fresh air was almost like being released from prison, although she had thought enough to remain back in the shadows until she decided on her next move. She was in, but the most difficult part of her errand still lay ahead of her, and she had to admit to not having the slightest idea how to go about finding Yusuf ben Dacra, let alone passing on the group's message.

She stood at one end of a large patio that was not quite square, and the high walls on this side were draped with curtains of purple bougainvillea and shadowed by the fern-like spread of jacarandas that stirred lightly in the wind. The patio was bordered on three sides by flowers that overflowed on to the paved surface and spilled blooms of every conceivable colour in riotous extravagance, while in the centre of it all an enormous fountain tinkled and splashed into a wide stone basin.

It was a delightful place and at any other time Lisa would have paused to enjoy it; now she could think of nothing but the errand she had been entrusted with. She still could not recognise either excitement or fear for certain, but suspected that it was a mingling of the two that made her feel slightly sick as she stood there hesitating.

'Bonsoir, mademoiselle!'

Lisa swung round quickly and was so obviously startled that the young man who had spoken raised a curious brow. 'I—I'm sorry,' she whispered, hastily gathering her wits together. 'I didn't see you there.'

'Ah! You are English—I had assumed you to be French.' He used slim brown hands to suggest her slender shape and his eyes skimmed over her approvingly. 'So—*chic*, eh?'

Lisa smiled. It was impossible not to after such a

compliment, and he had the kind of face that women would always smile at. He was about twenty-five or six and darkly handsome as so many Moroccans were, but to Lisa he was also a possible ally. As a guest at the Sheik's party he would almost certainly know the man she sought, even if only by sight. She had hoped to remain undetected for a little longer, but perhaps it was as well to be plunged into the task before she had time to see too many drawbacks and lose her nerve.

But her obvious uneasiness must have puzzled him, for he was eyeing her with a hint of speculation that suggested he was less blithely offhand than he appeared. 'You appear to be somewhat uneasy,' he said. 'Surely you have not been deserted by your partner? Some men are such fools that it is hard to credit their foolishness!'

Lisa shook her head. 'Oh no, I haven't been deserted.'

Obviously more intrigued than ever, he cocked his dark head to one side and studied her for a second. 'You are not here alone! I will not believe that you have come here alone—no man worthy of the name would allow such a state of affairs!'

In other circumstances, Lisa guessed, she would have enjoyed flirting with him, for he was a very attractive man, but she had other things on her mind at the moment, so she simply smiled a little absently. Not the kind of reception he was accustomed to, she suspected, but he drew one hand from his pocket and offered it with another smile.

'I am Yacub ben Abahn el Boudri,' he told her, and his expression assumed she would recognise his connection with the Sheik.

The fact that she had been discovered by one of the Sheik's family could be an advantage, but then again he could well prove less friendly once he knew why she was there. She shook his hand but refrained from telling him her own name because she preferred to keep her identity quiet at the moment. Instead she felt her way carefully.

'You're Sheik Abahn's son?' she guessed, and white teeth once more beamed in a smile.

'One of them,' he agreed. 'I am the youngest one, to be accurate; I have six brothers.' Probably counting his adopted brother, Yusuf ben Dacra, Lisa thought, once more charmed by that smile. 'But you are not interested in my brothers, eh? They are all married, except one, and I am not; not so far. That is in my favour, yes?'

'You speak very good English,' Lisa ventured, wanting to bring the subject round to Yusuf ben Dacra, but not quite knowing how to at the moment. 'Were you educated in England, Mr Boudri?'

'My father was, and four of my brothers.' He replied readily, but when he leaned back against the trunk of a jacaranda his eyes were as curious as they were appreciative. 'Also my adopted brother is something of a linguist and taught our young sister English, so that I feel I must not be outdone.'

It was the opening Lisa needed and she pounced on it. 'That's Yusuf ben Dacra?'

He was more intrigued than ever and the velvet-dark eyes quizzed her in their turn. 'You know Yusuf?' he asked.

Lisa's tongue flicked anxiously over her lips. 'As a matter of fact I came especially to see him,' she admitted, and Yacub Boudri's black brows arched swiftly in surprise. 'It's rather important that I see him tonight; I'd be very grateful if you'd point him out to me.'

'You have to see him on a matter of importance, and yet you do not know him even by sight?'

Lisa could understand his confusion, but she was so close now and she could not afford to let this chance slip away from her. 'I have something vital to say to him,' she pleaded, watching through her lashes to see what effect her appeal was having. 'It's a—a matter of business—urgent business.'

'So?' Lisa doubted very much if he believed her, and yet she had the feeling that he would, eventually, either point out Yusuf ben Dacra to her or take her in to see him. 'I admit to being intrigued,' he told her, still with a trace of a smile. 'I have never before known my brother to do business with a lovely young woman, it is not like him at all.' The bright, mischievous eyes swept over her flushed face and he smiled broadly again. 'But then perhaps this is not the customary type of business that Yusuf does, eh?'

'Oh, but it isn't anything like that——' Lisa stopped short, a flush warming her cheeks when she saw the way he was smiling. Perhaps she should have let him go on believing it was for sentimental reasons that she wanted to see Yusuf ben Dacra, then he would have been more ready to help her. But it was too late now, she had denied it too earnestly. 'I would be *very* grateful if you'd point him out to me,' she said, and Yacub Boudri nodded.

'Better than that,' he promised, and laid a hand on her arm. 'I will ask Yusuf to come out here and see you—on a matter of business, eh?' His sudden laughter suggested he did not for a moment believe she had anything as mundane as business in mind when she saw his brother, but that he was intrigued enough to play along. 'One thing I will warn you of,' he said, more soberly suddenly. 'If you *have* managed to fool me, you will not find Yusuf so easy; nor is he so tolerant of intruders, however lovely they are. You will remember that, eh?'

He was generous in the circumstances, Lisa thought, guessing she was there without an invitation, to let her know that his brother would be less tolerant. 'I'll remember,' she promised. 'Thank you.'

He gave a light shrug, as if he resigned himself to the fact that it was his adopted brother and not he in whom she was most interested, and Lisa watched him cross the patio towards the house. She was anxious but excited as well by the possibility of risk in the situation, and she took advantage of her breathing space to admire the garden.

It was breathtaking with its profusion of blossoms and scents, and it was rather surprising to realise that here in this walled garden, she was far more aware of the light of the moon than she had been in the street outside, despite the light coming from the house. It gave a softness and beauty to everything and sat like some benign god in the purple night sky above the trees.

Behind her was the tunnel-like passage by which she had come in only a very short time before, and growing beside it was a magnificent magnolia, its waxen blossoms gleaming white in the moonlight. It was irresistible to take the few steps necessary to bring her close to it, and she bent her head for a moment to inhale the perfume, everything else forgotten for a few seconds.

It was when she straightened up and glanced once more across the gardens that she realised she was about to meet Yusuf ben Dacra face to face, and she caught her breath sharply. The length and purposefulness of his stride made it obvious that he took as much exception to her message as Yacub Boudri had anticipated, and it was all she could do not to turn and disappear into that dark, cold passage again.

He had a certain air about him, an arrogance that matched the character she had already attributed to her quarry. Also he was tall and ruggedly masculine, with dark hair and eyes and a skin the colour of teak, and he held his head at an angle that emphasised the strong hawkishness of his profile as he skirted the stone basin of the fountain with long angry strides.

High cheekbones and an almost Roman nose combined with a firm straight mouth to suggest the harshness Lisa had been led to believe he was capable of. He wore a light blue shirt, and a white suit set off his darkness as well as emphasised the length of his legs and the leanness of his body. He looked like a man who would let nothing stand in his way, and knowing she was expected to tell him of the group's plans regarding his latest project, made Lisa quake inwardly.

He made the quite un-Moroccan gesture of dispensing with a polite greeting and came directly to the point, and Lisa guessed that his brother had also passed on the information that she was not an invited guest. 'I do not know who you are, *mademoiselle,*' he said in a deep and very attractive voice, 'but I demand to know for what reason you informed my brother that you had urgent business with me.'

His gaze was fierce and direct, and a few moments under its scrutiny made Lisa feel that she had been stripped naked and judged harshly, so that she needed to summon all her courage to say what she had to say. 'You are Yusuf ben Dacra?'

A curt nod confirmed what she already knew. 'You have no connection with either my business or my private life,' he told her. 'I therefore assume that you have some ulterior motive for seeking me out, *mademoiselle*. And since I am not in the habit of leaving important guests to answer mysterious summonses from unidentified females, you may count yourself lucky that I am simply ordering you off my father's property and not taking stronger action. Goodnight!'

Lisa passed the tip of her tongue across her lips in a gesture that was unconscious but revealing, and she spoke up quickly before he could turn away. 'I've been sent to warn you, Yusuf ben Dacra!'

The dark eyes narrowed slightly, glittering with contempt but curious too. 'You have been sent to *warn* me?' He swept his gaze over her in a swift explicit survey that aroused every nerve in her body. '*You* have been sent to warn *me*?'

'If you'll just give me chance to say what I came to say——' Lisa began, but was cut short by the dismissive gesture of one big hand.

'I have not the slightest desire to listen to anything you may have to say, *mademoiselle*, and you will leave at once by the same method in which you entered, or I shall take appropriate steps to have you removed!'

Too staggered for a moment to say anything, Lisa stared at him, but when he half-turned and would have left her, she spoke up, her temper flaring and her eyes gleaming determinedly. 'I haven't——'

Once more the relentless voice cut her short, bull-dozing her into silence. 'Do you deny that you entered by way of the street door?' he demanded, and reached out to take a handful of soft yellow silk, the pull of his strong fingers exerting so much force that the scarf was snatched from her head. Thrusting it on to her notice, he showed her a streak of damp mould that must have come from the chill walls of the passageway. 'You are an interloper, and if you are not gone from here within the next few seconds you will see the inside of a police cell!'

Lisa was trembling, but not altogether with fear, she realised. She was angry and also oddly excited, a mood that she was at a complete loss to understand. 'You can't have me arrested simply because I came in uninvited,' she declared, and blinked when she caught a brief glimpse of something other than anger in the dark eyes for a moment. 'I won't leave until——'

She let out a cry of alarm when hard strong fingers closed tightly about her upper arm and she was half dragged, half led round to the entrance of the narrow tunnel. Struggling against the bruising grip and stumbling in her haste, she was hauled unceremoniously along the gloomy passage to the gate, making vague, indignant threats in a breathlessly small voice.

Inside there was no glimmer of light showing as there had been when she came in, and she was alone in the close confines of the cold walls and low roof with a man who obviously had no qualms about manhandling a woman. He was silent, but it was a furious silence, and the lean, angry body striding beside her bumped her against the stone walls as they went.

Then the door opened, just far enough for her slender form to be pushed through into the street with sufficient force to send her staggering right across the narrow footpath. Breathless and bewildered, she heard the dull echo of the heavy wooden door being closed firmly, and the sound of a key being turned. It was too late by the time she noticed that her scarf had been pulled from her shoulders when she was thrust out into the street, and it was caught irretrievably between the door and its frame, trailing down on to the path like a streak of yellow paint.

Taken by surprise by her sudden appearance as he was, it took Geoffrey a moment or two to realise what had happened and in the ensuing silence Lisa heard the faintest echo of firm footsteps going back along the passageway. Recovering hastily, Geoffrey came around to join her, taking her protectively into his arms while he looked down into her flushed face.

She was still trembling, but she believed it was with anger rather than any other emotion, and she looked up at him with a rueful smile.

'I muffed it,' she confessed, and Geoffrey gazed at her anxiously. Somehow, she thought, his handsome features looked strangely pallid after the teak-dark fierceness of Yusuf ben Dacra.

'Are you all right?' he asked. 'What happened, Lisa? Did they find you too soon?'

Recollection made her more angry than ever, and when she considered the cavalier way she had been tossed out into the street, her determination to stop him having his way with the village of Zobi was stronger than ever it had been. The battle with Yusuf ben Dacra was a personal thing now and she would see it through to the bitter end.

'He threw me out this time,' she told Geoffrey with a gleam in her blue eyes. 'But I've no intention of letting him get away with it—I'll make him listen to me one way or another!'

'I don't like the idea,' Geoffrey muttered, and Lisa surprised herself by feeling a twinge of impatience with his caution.

'You don't have to,' she told him, brushing down her dress before she got back into the car. 'Tackling Yusuf ben Dacra is *my* part in the plan, and I'll find some way of getting to him, I promise you!'

CHAPTER TWO

It would make things so much easier, Lisa thought, if she knew just when Yusuf ben Dacra intended starting on the destruction of Zobi to make way for his luxury hotel. She was annoyed with herself for failing the previous evening, and especially when she had been face to face with the man, but he had been so different from what she expected. True, he had proved just as hard and unfeeling as she had been led to believe, but she was forced to recognise that there was something more to him than that. Something that aroused other emotions than anger, and his forceful handling of the situation last night had put her completely off her stroke.

Just the same, a night's sleep had done nothing to diminish her determination, and while she finished her breakfast coffee she mused on other ways to get to Yusuf ben Dacra. Every so often, and quite unconsciously, one hand strayed to her left arm where his hard fingers had left their impression, and whenever she remembered her humiliating exit from Sheik Abahn's property she was more determined than ever to make up for her failure.

Geoffrey was always busy during the day, at the Embassy in Rabat, and she was never very keen on joining the rest of the group unless he was with her, so that she had decided to drive a little way along the coast on her own, and try to think up an alternative plan for tackling Yusuf ben Dacra. Driving always seemed to aid her thought processes, and she never tired of the view from the coast road.

It was scorchingly hot as she drove along Boulevard

Sour Djedid towards the P2 coastal highway, but as soon as she got out of town and on to the *corniche* it was different. There was a light wind off the water that came in through the open window of her car and cooled her face and arms while she admired the scenery.

Rocky cliffs strode downward to the sea and stood with their feet in Atlantic rollers that foamed and pounded themselves to destruction in a shower of rainbow spray. It held a fascination for Lisa that she could never quite explain, but made it almost compulsory for her to come back to it again and again.

Not very far out of town there was a spot she had found quite by accident, where it was possible, with care, to drive some way off the road and on to a kind of rocky lay-by. An unofficial one, it was true, and not the kind of place many drivers would care to take their cars, but familiarity had perhaps made Lisa less wary than she had been on her first visit.

As long as she stopped short of where the rocks sloped steeply to the sea, it was safe enough, she felt, and she could sit just a little further on and look down in solitary grandeur at the endless pounding of the Atlantic. It was a splendid place to relax, she knew from experience.

Perhaps it was taking a chance to drive over such a rocky surface, and especially so close to the brink, but she had done so until now without incurring disaster, although the springs of her ancient car protested warningly. There was no one else about when she turned off the road, only a couple of vague figures in the distance driving a cart of some kind, and she slowed almost to a standstill as she prepared for the first shock of driving on to the rocks. Even so she gritted her teeth against the jolting bumps that seemed to jar every bone in her body, while reminding herself not to go too dangerously close to the sheer drop that plunged down to the sea.

'Idiot!'

The expletive was made in response to a sudden jarring lurch when one of the front wheels hit a larger rock than usual and the steering-wheel was snatched from her hands. But self-recrimination became a sudden cry of alarm when she realised the car was veering towards a large rock that loomed ahead, and that she was virtually helpless to do anything but shift her foot hastily to the footbrake.

What happened next Lisa had no clear idea, for the sudden application of the brake had thrown her forward and brought her head into brief contact with the edge of the windscreen. She lost consciousness and slumped across the steering-wheel, lost to the world for a few moments and completely unaware of what was going on around her.

The first thing she became aware of was the sound of men's voices, and that only in a vague and indistinct way at first. They were speaking Arabic, that much her fuddled brain registered after a few seconds, and one voice in particular seemed to be more audible than the other, as if the owner of it was closer to her.

Hands moved across her forehead, anxiously clumsy hands that probably were meant to be soothing but instead alarmed her, because she could not for the moment think what had happened to her. Her head ached and her eyelids felt much too heavy to open, nor could she seem to stop herself from drifting into occasional moments of oblivion.

Then she felt the sun on her face suddenly, as if whoever had been bending over her had moved aside, and amid the murmur of voices she caught the word *effendi*, then a short silence. She was still unable to rouse herself sufficiently to open her eyes, but she began to register and to recognise certain facts.

Like the fact that someone was once more bending

over her, when the sun's heat was cut off again and her face was in cool shade. And that the basic, masculine smell of her first attendant had been replaced by the tangy sophistication of an expensive brand of French after-shave.

Then once more exploratory fingers moved across her brow at the hairline, but this time the touch was more assured, as well as firm but gentle. Lisa gave an involuntary moan when the fingers touched a spot more tender than the rest and again wafted off into semi-consciousness before she could decide why there was something oddly familiar about the proximity of the new arrival.

When next she became aware of anything it was to find herself being carried in a pair of strong arms, while her head lolled against the comforting solidity of a masculine shoulder. There was something so infinitely reassuring about the situation that she was content to let it go on for the moment. Her face turned from the heat of the sun and her cheek pressed to what she was becoming increasingly aware was the softness of a freshly laundered shirt, warmed by the masculine body it covered.

He must have been very strong, for he held her easily, whoever he was. '*Mademoiselle?*'

The voice struck an immediate chord; deep and quiet and extraordinarily attractive, and Lisa was not quite sure whether the moan she gave when she recognised it was audible or not. Her eyelids fluttered but her eyes remained closed and she tucked her face more firmly into the hollow of his shoulder.

The last time she had heard that voice it had been threatening to have her thrown into a police cell if she did not leave Sheik Abahn's garden at once, and she had no desire to face Yusuf ben Dacra again at the moment. Voices murmured again and a few moments later she was laid with infinite care on to what felt like a comfortable bed.

One hand kept her head from lolling sideways again while long fingers stroked the hair from her forehead with slow gentle movements. But Lisa kept her eyes closed still rather than look into those relentlessly fierce features she remembered so well, and which seemed to be hovering above her, judging by the proximity of his voice.

'*Mademoiselle*, try to open your eyes, please!'

The voice once more broke insistently into her lethargy, and Lisa obeyed it almost instinctively, raising her heavy lids as far as it was possible at the moment, and looking up at him with the vagueness of semi-consciousness still veiling her eyes. Both the hand on her brow and the one supporting her head were withdrawn the moment he realised she was conscious, and he eased himself back from a rather awkward kneeling position beside the car seat she lay on. *His* car obviously, since it was large and opulent and smelled of new leather and that distinctive French after-shave.

He ducked back through the car door and stood looking down at her for a moment, and with the harsh Moroccan sun behind him and the indistinct shapes of a couple of men in traditional country garb behind him he looked curiously unreal for a moment. Then he ducked his head inside again and eyed her with only a little less fierceness than last night. His mouth was firm and straight, as if he saw the necessity of coming to her aid as just another attempt to annoy him.

'I am pleased to see that you are recovered, *mademoiselle*,' he said in the impeccable English Geoffrey had remarked on. 'Your vehicle, unfortunately, is in a much worse condition. Do you feel able to sit up?'

Lisa had little option to decide for herself, for he knelt between the front and back seats and slid an arm under her shoulders, raising her from the soft leather seat and bringing her into closer proximity with himself. He had no jacket on, and the pale fawn shirt he wore fitted his muscular frame like a second skin, showing the shadow of teak-brown skin through its fine texture and a slash of brown throat at the open neck. He was an infinitely disturbing man at such close quarters, she found, and she quite inexplicably resented the fact.

Apparently assuming that she was capable of sitting up alone, he moved back to stand outside again, and Lisa was able to take better stock of him without being distracted by his physical nearness. Fawn trousers exactly matched the open-necked shirt and fitted over lean hips and powerful-looking legs, as he stood looking in at her, but he lost none of his arrogance, or his suggestion of power, for being casually dressed. He was every bit as impressive in daylight as he had been in Sheik Abahn's garden last night, and no less overwhelming.

It was Lisa who broke the silence because she found it much too discomfiting in the circumstances, and because that steady dark gaze seemed to express something much different from polite sympathy. 'I'm not sure what happened,' she ventured, and the answer came unhesitatingly; as uncompromising as she should have expected from him.

'It appears that you drove off the road and on to the rocks quite deliberately, *mademoiselle*,' he informed her, leaving her in no doubt that he believed it. 'These two men were not too far away and they saw it happen.' The dark eyes held hers steadily and she did her best not to let her own waver and give way. 'They are of the opinion that you must be suffering from too much sun,' he added, 'and it is an opinion I find myself having to agree with, since I cannot imagine anyone in her right mind attempting to drive a car on to such a surface.'

'Well, you're wrong!' Lisa declared swiftly and indignantly. But indignation and the sudden upward jerk of her head sent a jarring pain searing across her brow and she looked at him as reproachfully as if he had been personally responsible for it, while she clasped a hand to her aching head. 'I've driven off the road at that point several times before, and parked my car, without anything like this happening.'

'Then you have been very fortunate,' Yusuf ben Dacra decreed without hesitation. 'Did you never stop to consider the danger of such an action?' Lisa said nothing, but kept her eyes lowered, feeling more sorry for herself than ever because there was so little she could say in her own defence. 'You are also very fortunate not to have been more seriously hurt in this instance; you could very easily have ended your life on the rocks below there.'

Lisa resented his lecturing her, mostly because she knew that what he said was right, though she had no intention of admitting it and giving him the satisfaction. She felt tremblingly unsteady and she wanted sympathy, not condemnation, though it was unlikely to be forthcoming from this man. A guarded, upward glance showed impatience in the dark watching eyes, not sympathy, and she made another attempt to justify her actions.

'I've managed perfectly well until now,' she insisted huskily. 'I just happened to be unlucky this time and hit a rock, that's all.'

'It would be difficult to do otherwise, driving over a surface that consists entirely of rocks,' he remarked with undisguised contempt, and Lisa realised that the two men watching were taking an increasing interest in what they were saying. Whether or not they spoke any English it must be fairly evident that the conversation between herself and Yusuf ben Dacra verged on a quarrel. 'Whatever the cause,' he went on, 'the result is that you now have no car.'

He made the observation without a hint of sympathy and Lisa, with a hand to her throbbing head, looked at him uncertainly. It was maddening to feel so helpless when she normally considered herself such an independent woman, and it seemed, having rescued her, Yusuf ben Dacra was in no hurry to offer further assistance.

She felt curiously isolated too, with the three men standing as they were in a group, for it made her feel as if they were all in league and had unanimously decided that she was a headstrong female who suddenly found herself out of her depth. Watched by three pairs of dark eyes, she swung her legs off the seat and edged towards the door, wondering how on earth she was going to bring herself to ask Yusuf ben Dacra's help in getting home.

She would probably have managed to get out of the car alone even though her legs felt so unsteady, but no sooner had she put her feet to the ground than her hands were grasped by two large strong ones that drew her up from the seat and steadied her for a moment. It was for only a few seconds, but Lisa was appalled by how urgently her pulses responded while his strong fingers were curled about hers, engulfing them in a firm masculine warmth that sent shivers of sensation shivering along her spine.

When he released her his fingers seemed to slide away with an almost sensual slowness that startled her. 'You have only a slight injury to your forehead,' he informed her. 'It is nothing that needs medical attention, but you are very fortunate indeed to have escaped so lightly.'

'So you've already said!' The retort was irresistible, although Lisa knew she was being very ungracious in the circumstances. When she put an exploratory hand to her head she caught her breath, for it proved more painful than she expected, and she wondered if he was deliberately underplaying her injuries. There was a bump just near the hairline and the skin was grazed. 'It hurts a lot, even if it isn't very bad,' she told him. 'I must have hit my head on the windscreen when I braked.'

'It would seem so,' Yusuf ben Dacra concurred. 'You were unconscious when I arrived, although these men had lifted you from the car and laid you on the ground in what little shade they could find. It was little enough, but they did what they could.'

'And I'm grateful to them.' It came back to her then, and Lisa felt a new and disturbing response to the recollection of being carried in his arms. Of the reassuring strength of them and of the sensation of a warm masculine body pressed to her cheek. 'You carried me to your car,' she said, with unaccustomed meekness. 'That was very kind of you.'

From his expression she gathered that her thanks were something he could well have managed without, and he brushed them aside with the merest suggestion of a nod. 'It was necessary to move you into more shade,' he told her shortly, 'and my car offered the most comfortable alternative.'

'Thank you anyway.'

Her hands strayed once more to her head and she winced involuntarily when her fingers touched the slight bump. It probably felt much worse than it looked, she realised, but she was still slightly muzzy-headed and she was beginning to wonder how she was going to get home unless it was with his help—something that his present attitude seemed to suggest was unlikely.

'I seem to be in rather a predicament, don't I?' she said, and smiled a little warily while trying to judge his reaction through half-lowered lashes.

There was nothing in the dark-eyed gaze to encourage

her, only a hint of impatience, and for a moment she wondered if he really would leave her there to make her own way back without any further assistance from him. 'Do you live in Casablanca, *mademoiselle?*' Lisa nodded cautiously. 'Then of course you will drive back with me.'

Lisa was imagining the drive back, side by side with the man she had gone to so much trouble to see last night, and she found herself unable to anticipate it without a certain tingle of excitement. 'That's very kind of you, Mr ben Dacra,' she said, as coolly as she was able, 'if you're sure it won't be out of your way.'

'You are aware of the fact that I live in Casablanca, *mademoiselle*,' he reminded her. 'And unless you are prepared to wait out here for a taxi to collect you, or you are proposing to walk home, I see no alternative. Your car is out of action and in any case you are not in a fit state to drive yourself at the moment.'

If only he had sounded more enthusiastic about it, Lisa would have felt better, but she supposed a grudging offer of help was better than none at all, and she nodded vague agreement with his reasoning without saying anything. She was thinking what an opportunity it would have been in other circumstances to remedy her failure last night, but she could hardly make threats to a man who was helping her.

As it was her reticence must have given him the wrong idea, for he regarded her frowningly when she did no more than nod in response to his suggestion, and when she glanced at him she realised what a contradictory creature he must think her. Last night she had been prepared to risk being locked in a cell to see him, and today she showed little enthusiasm for the prospect of driving back to Casablanca with him.

'When you have made up your mind whether or not you will accompany me, *mademoiselle*,' he said with a hint of sarcasm, 'perhaps we can be on our way.'

'Oh yes, of course.' She pulled herself hastily together. 'I'll be very grateful for a lift home, thank you.'

'On one condition!' Lisa looked up quickly, and immediately regretted the effect it had on her aching head. 'I have no intention of becoming a captive audience,' he warned. 'If you attempt to deliver whatever warning you mentioned last night at my father's house, I shall have not the slightest compunction in stopping the car and putting you out. Is that understood? If I drive you to your home it is only on the understanding that you behave with more courtesy than you did last night when you forced your way into our property uninvited.'

Having already decided that doing as he suggested was out of the question in the circumstances, Lisa took exception to his warning, and made no effort to conceal the fact. Her face flushed with warm colour, she looked up at him with a sparkle of indignation in her eyes and her chin at an angle, despite her throbbing head.

'We were both lacking courtesy last night, Mr ben Dacra,' she said, her voice slightly shaky. 'You have no cause to suggest that my manners are any worse than yours, just because I had a very good reason for acting as I did last time we met.'

He took her reproach narrow-eyed and there was a tight firmness about his mouth that suggested to Lisa that beneath that smoothly confident manner of his there lurked a quite formidable temper. He held her gaze for a moment and with such unmistakable scorn that it was she who eventually yielded and lowered her eyes.

He turned and opened the front passenger seat door, indicating that she should get in, and while she hesitated for just a moment, he said something to the two men just behind him. They glanced at Lisa while he spoke and she guessed he was explaining as much of the outcome as he thought necessary. Then the one who seemed to be the spokesman for them both inclined his turbanned head slightly in her direction and murmured something in Arabic, before turning to follow his companion.

Even in their dusty white *serwal* and simple shirts they had a curiously touching dignity, and they had come willingly to her aid apparently, so that she spoke up quickly before they walked out of earshot. 'I'd like to thank them for helping me,' she said, and looked to Yusuf ben Dacra to help her. 'Will you do that for me, please?'

He nodded shortly, then called after the two men in their own tongue. They turned slowly and listened to what he had to say, then gravely inclined their heads, murmuring deprecation of their own attempts to help her, before once more going on their way. Watching them go, Lisa almost started visibly when she felt a hand under her arm, urging her into the passenger seat, and she looked up into the dark, impatient face of Yusuf ben Dacra.

She yielded to its persuasion after one brief rueful glance at her own small car, crumpled and useless against the rock she had inadvertently driven into. Settled into the deep comfort of soft leather, she found it hard not to relax, and she glanced from the corner of her eye at him when he slid into the seat beside her.

He must have noticed her expression when she saw her own car and as he started the engine he too glanced across at the wreck. 'You see how fortunate you were not to be much more seriously injured, *mademoiselle*,' he said. Lisa did not reply, having remarked on his persistent reminders of the fact already, and he went on, 'I doubt very much if your car is worth recovering, but probably you will wish to notify a garage when you return in case something can be salvaged from the wreck.'

Lisa had a genuine affection for her old car, though she doubted very much if a man like Yusuf ben Dacra would appreciate such a sentiment. Nevertheless she expressed her own regret in the words that came to her instinctively. 'I was very fond of old Lizzie,' she said, and caught his swift sideways glance from the corner of her eye.

'Then you will no doubt wish to have it repaired if it is at all possible,' he said, and quite unexpectedly she detected sympathy for her sentimental attachment. 'If you approach Omar el Idris, who is to be found just off the Rue Tarik, it is possible he can help you. If he says that there is nothing to be done then you may be certain there *is* nothing to be done; he is the best mechanic in Casablanca.'

Startled into silence for a moment or two by his ready offer of assistance, Lisa felt the steady, urgent beat of her heart as they gathered speed along the coast road. The last thing she expected from him, on any matter at all, was co-operation, and she found it curiously affecting.

'Then I'll certainly try him,' she said after a moment or two, and glanced once more at the strong dark profile of the man beside her. 'Thank you.'

Dark eyes turned briefly in her direction and she felt the hard thudding beat her heart gave. *'Pas de quoi, mademoiselle,'* he said, and it did not yet strike Lisa as odd that when he resorted to another language suddenly it was French rather than his native Arabic.

It was pure chance that took Lisa to the Bab restaurant, for she had meant only to do a little shopping and then return home for lunch. Instead she had taken a lot longer over her shopping than she planned and then found herself feeling too tired to go in search of a taxi. Her head was pounding like a drum and reminding her that only the day before yesterday she had been involved in an accident, and would probably have been wiser to take longer over her recovery.

It did not really matter that she chose to have lunch in the nearest restaurant instead of going home to the solitary lunch left for her. For her father was away on one of his frequent business trips, and Madame Raymond, their French-Moroccan housekeeper, was visiting her sister-in-law for the day. Her time was her own.

The Bab was a restaurant she knew only by reputation because it was one she normally considered outside her pocket, but today would have to be the exception. It was large and fairly new, but thoroughly traditional in its decor, and Lisa hoped as she settled at her table that she had enough money left to pay the bill when it came.

Beautiful Moorish arches divided the huge room into sections and these again were sub-divided by tall palms planted in ornate stone urns and making private and intriguing little corners everywhere. The walls were lined with a type of cubicle formed by filigree screens of Moorish design, and she had one of these to herself, as it was early yet by Moroccan standards.

The food was excellent, and she was sipping a final cup of thick black coffee when she became aware that someone was taking the table next to hers, on the other side of the screen. She heard the shuffling of feet as they were seated, and the murmured pleasantries of the waiter and then an English voice, unmistakably North-Country but with the broad vowels smoothed over and flattened.

It was when his companion replied to a question of choice from the menu, however, that Lisa's attention was caught, and she listened without being fully aware that she was doing so. She identified the second voice without hesitation as Yusuf ben Dacra's, deep and attractive and unmistakable, and she wondered why she felt so suddenly alert and self-conscious. The Englishman seemed to be dominating the conversation so far, but something he said made Lisa catch her breath and listen unashamedly for the answer.

'What's this I hear about an hotel at Zobi?'

The confident voice left her in no doubt that she had heard the question correctly, and she waited with bated breath to hear what Yusuf ben Dacra said in reply. In his quiet, faultless English he gave his companion a brief outline of his scheme to build the biggest and most luxurious hotel along the Atlantic coast of Morocco, and Lisa heard every word above the thuddingly heavy beat of her heart.

'I shall be sailing down there tomorrow or the following day to oversee the initial stages,' he concluded, and satisfaction was evident in his voice, 'after that I shall leave it in the hands of my manager, Abdullah.'

'You're taking that yacht of yours, I suppose?' the Englishman guessed with undisguised envy. 'The *Djenoun*, isn't it? You lucky devil, I really envy you that craft, Yusuf. I'd give my right arm for something like her.'

'She is beautiful,' Yusuf agreed, 'but like a beautiful woman, she is sometimes difficult to handle.' Although she had never actually seen him smile, Lisa could imagine it. It would be a wide, dazzling smile, she thought; a slash of white in that teak-brown face. 'I am fortunate to be able to make use of her in this instance,' he went on, blandly unaware of an eavesdropper. 'I have the time to sail down to Zobi instead of driving, which would be much quicker but much less enjoyable. I like to combine business with pleasure whenever possible.'

He sounded so cool and confident, so certain that nothing and no one could prevent him from doing exactly as he wanted that Lisa was very tempted to walk around the concealing screen that divided the two tables and confront him. She longed to tell him what the group had in store for him if he went ahead with his precious plans, but instead she simply finished her coffee, then called over the waiter with her bill.

It appalled her to realise that she was trembling when she got to her feet, and there was no way of leaving the restaurant without him seeing her, for he was seated facing outwards into the room. A swift elevation of his black brows signalled his recognition of her and Lisa was unsure how to react, so she quickly lowered her eyes after that first glance and hoped he would let it go at that.

But he apparently had no intention of ignoring her, and he rose to his feet as she drew level with his table, and inclined his head slightly, his eyes narrowed against the smoke from a long black Kébir. '*Mademoiselle.*' His hint of a bow was impeccably polite. 'I hope you are recovered from your accident?'

When he got to his feet, his companion followed suit and was eyeing her with undisguised curiosity. The injury was concealed by a swathe of sun-bleached hair, but she automatically put a hand to her forehead and exposed the place, grimacing in a way that gave lie to her answer. 'Yes, perfectly recovered, thank you, Mr ben Dacra.'

He could quite clearly see the evidence for himself and he noted the still visible swelling above her right eye and the dark smudge of bruise with a slight frown. 'Not yet perfectly, I think,' he said, and Lisa guessed that insistence on absolute accuracy was part and parcel of his character. 'It is obvious that you still have bruises and there is some swelling still—you must have some discomfort from it, surely?'

'A headache, that's all.' She realised how oddly breathless she sounded, but she found his unexpected concern very disconcerting and she was not quite sure how to react to it. 'It's very kind of you to be so concerned, but I'm really quite recovered, thank you.'

Her almost meekly polite reply surprised her, but in the circumstances there was little else she could have said, and she was beginning to find the unconcealed interest of the man with him rather embarrassing. Once or twice he had cleared his throat, as if to draw attention to himself, but it took Lisa a moment or two to realise that, even had the informality of the occasion warranted an introduction, Yusuf ben Dacra did not know her name.

She clasped her parcels a little more firmly and summoned a smile that was just as uncertain as her voice, and prepared to leave. 'If you'll excuse me,' she said, 'I have to go and find a taxi to take me home.'

That would have been an end of it, and she could have simply walked off, leaving the two of them to their lunch, but it was obvious that the Englishman had every intention of discovering who she was before she left. He beamed her a broad, confident smile and caught her unwilling eye as she started to leave.

'You're very obviously a countrywoman of mine,' he said, and thrust out a hand it was difficult to ignore. 'I'm from Bradford, but you come from somewhere further south, I'd guess, eh?' Lisa nodded without specifying a particular place. 'My name's Sam Martin, and it doesn't look as if my friend here is going to introduce me, so I'd better do it myself. How'd you do?'

Lisa had no option but to take the proffered hand, and to give him her name, but she did so reluctantly. She had no real wish for Yusuf ben Dacra to be too well informed about her. 'Lisa Pelham,' she said. 'How do you do, Mr Martin?'

The large hand retained its hold and Lisa felt the sudden intensity of Yusuf's interest. 'Pelham?' The loud hearty voice repeated her name and bright curious eyes quizzed her shrewdly. 'You wouldn't be John Pelham's daughter, by any chance, would you?'

Lisa nodded, convinced of Yusuf ben Dacra's growing interest. 'Yes, I am,' she said. 'My father's over here as an industrial adviser to the Moroccan government.'

'So I heard.' Her hand was released at last and there was no concealing the fact that the jovially hearty voice was less friendly suddenly. 'He's been luckier than some of us, damned if he hasn't. I knew him before he attained such dizzying heights.'

'Mr Pelham holds a very important position,' Yusuf ben Dacra's voice confirmed it, but there was something about his manner suddenly that made Lisa uneasy, though she could not explain why. 'Our government values him highly.'

Lisa could just see a waiter from the corner of her eye, and she thought he was coming in their direction. She hoped he was, for she felt an urgent desire to get away from there, and his arrival was as good an opportunity as any. 'If you'll excuse me,' she said, and this time no one delayed her longer than it took Sam Martin to grasp her hand once more and shake it briefly.

'I hope we can meet again soon, Miss Pelham.' He glanced at Yusuf, tall and dark and very much at home against the exotic Moroccan background, and his eyes sparkled with a hint of malice. 'Maybe you'll be at the Sheik's next party?' he suggested. 'Or maybe Yusuf means to keep you out of reach of that handsome younger brother of his, eh?'

Lisa had seldom felt more embarrassed in her life, and she dared not look at Yusuf ben Dacra again. Instead she hastily took her leave of both men, her smile a little forced but outwardly cool, she hoped. 'Goodbye, Mr Martin, I'll tell my father I've met you. Goodbye, Mr ben Dacra.'

She merely glimpsed at the brief bow he gave as she

turned swiftly and made her way through the other tables to the door, but she heard the Englishman laugh loud and heartily when she was nearly half way across the room. Heaven knew what misconception he had about her relationship with Yusuf ben Dacra, and it was even more interesting to speculate on what Yusuf might say by way of an explanation.

He must know that she had overheard at least some of his conversation, but she doubted if that would trouble him much, for his plan to demolish Zobi was fairly common knowledge by now. What she did wonder was whether or not he would realise that his plans were what she had tried to warn him about. In any event, she thought she knew a way of getting to him now, and she stopped outside for a moment to mull it over briefly in her mind.

The idea had come to her when she heard Yusuf ben Dacra say that he intended sailing down the coast to Zobi in his own yacht, and it had taken firmer root even while she was talking to him and his friend. But she was not yet sure enough of it to grasp it unhesitatingly, and she was still unsure when she had dinner with Geoffrey that evening, although her conviction was growing.

At the moment she was still explaining how she came to have a bump on her forehead and a quite noticeable bruise, and she had got as far as admitting to having an accident with her car and to being rescued by Yusuf ben Dacra. His reaction was rather more dramatic than she expected, and she wished in a way she need not have told him.

'But why on earth wasn't I told about it?' Geoffrey demanded, and a certain suggestion of possessiveness in his tone made her frown.

'I didn't see the need,' she told him, deliberately off-hand. 'I simply had a minor mishap and Yusuf ben Dacra brought me home, that's all.'

'That's all, she says!' Geoffrey raised his eyes appealingly to heaven. 'You ought to take more care in that old jalopy of yours, Lisa, it's lethal.'

'Not any more,' Lisa told him with genuine regret. 'I tried the man that Yusuf ben Dacra said was the best mechanic in Casa, and he's told me that poor old Lizzie is a write-off—not even worth anything as scrap.'

'Well, it's just as well in my opinion,' Geoffrey said unfeelingly. 'It was a menace to life and limb and I never had a moment's peace while I knew you were riding around in it. What puzzles me is how ben Dacra got involved in it. Did you collide with him?'

'No, I didn't!' Lisa used her fork to seek out a particular morsel of chicken from the delicious concoction on her plate, and chose not to meet his eyes at that moment. 'I don't exactly know *how* he got involved,' she confessed. 'I gathered he was passing by and saw the other men there, but I don't really know because I was unconscious at the time. It goes without saying that the two country-type men who were apparently first on the scene took a back seat once Yusuf ben Dacra arrived, and he took charge.'

Geoffrey was once more shaking his head in despair. 'Oh, Lisa, my dear child, the chances you take!'

Geoffrey was nearly thirty and Lisa seven years his junior, but she disliked his rather patronising way of addressing her and let him know it. 'I don't take any more chances than anyone else,' she insisted firmly, 'and I object to being addressed as your dear child, Geoffrey. You're not old enough to be my father, and it makes you sound very pompous!'

'I'm sorry.'

His expression made her realise how sharp she had been, and she was immediately contrite. Reaching over, she pressed his hand and looked up into his face appealingly. 'No, *I'm* sorry, Geoffrey. That was very bitchy of me, and you don't deserve it.'

He said nothing for a moment, then he looked across at her and smiled ruefully, his grey eyes sober as always. 'Maybe I did deserve it,' he allowed, then shook his head and hastily changed the subject. 'I suppose you didn't take advantage of his driving you home to tell him what we have in store for him if he goes ahead with his scheme at Zobi, did you?'

Lisa frowned. 'How could I?' she asked. 'You don't accept someone's help and then turn around and threaten him with the disruption of his plans if he doesn't do as you tell him to.' She kept her eyes on the food in front of her rather than look at him still. 'Anyway, he said that if I as much as mentioned whatever it was I tried to warn him about the other night, he'd stop the car and throw me out. And remembering the way he flung me bodily into the street without a second thought the last time we met, I wasn't prepared to take the chance. I was in no state to walk home to Casa at the time.'

'Good heavens!' Geoffrey stared at her with his fork held inches from his open mouth. 'You don't honestly believe he meant it?'

'I'm quite sure he did!' Lisa declared unhesitatingly.

'I know he's reputed to be a hard man,' Geoffrey objected, 'but honestly, Lisa, I can't see him doing anything as uncouth as that.'

'He certainly convinced me,' Lisa insisted, although at the same time she found it hard to forget how he had come to her aid instead of simply driving on when he discovered who she was. 'I wouldn't even try to make head or tail of a man like him, quite honestly.'

'Incidentally,' Geoffrey remarked casually, 'I've discovered a bit more about his mysterious background. According to one of our chaps who's better informed than I am, he *is* part European. His father was French, though ben Dacra himself was born here and he's a Moroccan national.'

Lisa was interested, and she made no secret of the fact. Pushing aside her empty plate, she folded her arms on the table in front of her. 'I'd never have known it,' she mused, recalling almost black eyes, and the teak-brown skin through the thinness of a cream shirt. 'Was he——'

She raised a delicate brow rather than ask the question outright, and Geoffrey shrugged. 'All quite above board, apparently,' he told her. 'At least he has the Arabic version of his father's name. He was Joseph d'Acra, so I've been told, though as far as anyone knows the son is named Yusuf, not Joseph. The mother's influence, probably.' He seemed to notice the vaguely absent look in Lisa's eye then, and frowned at her curiously. 'Lisa, what's going on in that devious mind of yours?'

She did not take exception, but smiled instead, convinced in her own mind at last. 'I think I might have found a way of getting to him, Geoffrey, a way of getting our message over to him. Always providing I have the necessary nerve, of course.' Geoffrey was regarding her suspiciously. 'Did you know that he owns a yacht?' she asked. 'It's a very beautiful yacht, apparently, called the *Djenoun*. Did you know that?'

'Yes, I know it.' He looked uneasy suddenly and admitted his knowledge cautiously. 'But I don't see what that has to do with anything.'

'Don't you?' Her heart was hammering wildly and the more she considered the plan she had in mind, the more convinced she was of its perfection. 'Where does he keeps it?' she asked, ignoring his frown for the moment. 'In the harbour here, at Casa?'

Obviously not at all happy about her enthusiasm, Geoffrey shrugged, his eyes narrowed and mistrustful. 'Yes, of course he keeps it here,' he said. 'But what are you leading up to, Lisa? Why should you be so interested in ben Dacra's yacht and where he keeps it?'

When Lisa giggled as she did it was from sheer nervous excitement, and her eyes were a bright sparkling blue between their thick lashes. 'Because I'm going to stow away on it!' she told him. 'I've thought about it for hours, and I'm sure I could do it.'

'Good grief!' Geoffrey stared at her in blank-eyed astonishment.

'Well, why not?' Lisa demanded, piqued because he was not showing more enthusiasm for the idea. 'I can catch him before he sails and *make* him listen to me. I can tell him exactly what he can expect if he goes ahead with his plans to destroy Zobi; before he sets sail to start the scheme.'

'For heaven's sake, Lisa!' Geoffrey leaned across the table, his grey eyes anxiously holding her evasive gaze, determined to impress her with the madness of what she planned to do. 'You can't go on board the man's yacht, Lisa. It isn't like going to Sheik Abahn's place where there were other people about. Suppose there's only him there and maybe a couple of tough crew members? Good grief, anything could happen to you. No, my dear, definitely not—I forbid it!'

Lisa ignored his authoritative tone, and tried not to see the anxiety in his eyes. She had set her mind on this way to tackle Yusuf ben Dacra now, and it would take a lot to swerve her from her course. Her hands clasped together in front of her, she mused on her chances of getting aboard the *Djenoun* without being seen.

'He said he was sailing either tomorrow or the day after,' she said. 'I should have to try both days to make sure I got the right one.'

'No, Lisa!' Geoffrey gripped her hands tightly, and his eyes had a desperate look, as if he realised he could not win but felt bound to try. 'I'll have to——'

'You don't have to do anything,' Lisa told him with a touch of impatience. 'Just stand by with the others in case he turns down the warning out of hand—as I suspect he will,' she added.

'Oh, Lisa!'

She could not help feeling sorry for making him look so unhappy, but it did not make her consider changing her mind. It was the best way of getting to Yusuf ben Dacra and she meant to try; in fact the idea of seeing the craft he obviously set such store by, was quite exciting when she considered it further. She took Geoffrey's hands in hers and spoke quietly and confidently, even though her heart was hammering hard at her ribs, and there was a bright gleam of anticipation in her eyes.

'It's very simple, Geoffrey. I get aboard his yacht, and I'm not fooling myself that that won't be the most difficult part, then I simply come out of hiding the moment he comes aboard, and tell him what I have to about our plans for stopping him destroying Zobi—then I walk ashore.'

'Lisa, Lisa, you make it sound so easy——'

'There's no doubt it *will* be difficult, but it isn't impossible, and I'm going to try.'

Geoffrey was shaking his head and there was a look in his eyes that brought warmth to her cheeks, for she had caught glimpses of it once or twice lately and it disturbed her without her being quite sure why. Folding her hands between his, he looked at her earnestly.

'I wish I had the right to be more firm with you,' he said, and pressed her fingers tightly. 'You're as headstrong as you are lovely, my dear, and it's a very dangerous combination.' He bent his head for just a second and brushed her finger-tips lightly with his lips. 'Please be careful,' he begged.

'Of course I will!'

Lisa thought she caught sight of something in his eyes for a moment that was more than he intended her to see, and her heart leaped alarmingly. She liked Geoffrey, but she wasn't in love with him and she would rather he did not fall in love with her at the moment. That look in his eyes suggested it would be all too easy to hurt him, and she hated the idea of doing that. Gently disengaging her hands, she smiled across at him, keeping her voice determinedly light.

'Don't worry, Geoffrey!' Her laughter was a little unsteady and she tossed back her hair in a gesture that was more anxious than defiant. 'After all, what can he do to me other than have me put ashore with a flea in my ear?'

Geoffrey was shaking his head slowly, and his grey eyes had a dark, unhappy look that she carefully avoided. 'That's what worries me most,' he said.

CHAPTER THREE

Lisa had never considered herself to be a nervous type, and yet the idea of coming face to face with Yusuf ben Dacra again and in these particular circumstances made her alarmingly jittery. Finding his yacht, *Djenoun*, had not been difficult even in Casablanca's crowded harbour, but getting aboard her as easily as she had, Lisa realised, was sheer fluke.

As far as she could tell when she eventually found the *Djenoun*'s berth, the only person on board her was a single crewman, and she spent a full ten minutes watching and waiting to see if anyone else appeared. No one did and all she saw was the one young man leaning on the rail and looking faintly bored. He might have noticed her there, but before he had time to take more serious interest, someone hailed him from a passing boat and he hurried eagerly across to the other side to exchange greetings, leaving the coast clear.

Quick to grasp the opportunity, Lisa had slipped aboard, holding her breath in case her reading of the situation had been at fault and someone else was below deck. The accommodation was sumptuous down there, and she spent a few minutes opening doors and looking for a likely place to conceal herself until Yusuf ben Dacra came aboard.

A large galley and several smallish cabins she dismissed as unsuitable, but she was struck immediately by the possibilities of a large and luxurious salon amidships. It had all the luxury and extravagance of a Moroccan palace and it struck her as the kind of setting that would fit Yusuf ben Dacra like a glove.

The rich red medallions of a Rabat carpet with its traditional floral borders harmonised perfectly with dark antique furniture, and even the exquisite grace of Moorish arches had been reproduced so that lacy filigree patterns caught reflected sunlight from the water through wide square windows. The walls were white, and long bench-like seats upholstered in bright fabrics provided seating, as well as more conventional chairs.

An ornately decorated folding screen fronted by potted palms concealed a section of the room evidently set apart for letter-writing, or perhaps Yusuf ben Dacra never fully let go of business affairs and he needed somewhere to work, even here. Immediately below a window was a small antique desk and a matching chair and, apart from one thing, the little private section of the room made an ideal place to conceal herself.

The window was a drawback, for she could be seen by anyone passing along the deck, and she was anxious not to be seen until the moment was right. In the circumstances Lisa settled for the rather cramped cover of the folding screen where its leaves zig-zagged into slightly deeper folds at the window end, and resigned herself to waiting with as much patience as she could.

She was tense with anticipation and shivering with mingled anxiety and excitement, and it was only a matter of minutes before she decided that this kind of activity was not really in her line at all. She was not cut out for this cloak-and-dagger secrecy and, had it not been much too late, she would have renounced her interest in the Zobi project and left it to the more militant members of the group.

So far it had been very quiet, but then she caught the sound of men's voices somewhere, and the sound of laughter followed by the padding of feet on the linoleum-covered floor of the passage outside. Then, just when she had steeled herself for activity, it became quiet once more and she let out her breath, with her hands to her mouth to smother the sound it made.

It must have been another fifteen or twenty minutes before she heard another, slightly louder voice, and when she heard it her heart gave a sudden jolt of anticipation. She heard it again a few seconds later and it sounded to be immediately outside the door, then the unmistakable sound of the door opening made her catch her breath. It closed again and a firm tread crossed the salon, and she knew without a moment's hesitation that Yusuf ben Dacra was just the other side of the screen. It was what she had waited for, and yet as she crouched there in the folds of the screen she had the wild inclination to run.

The remembered scent of that expensive French aftershave tickled her nose pleasantly, and her heart was banging away at her ribs with the force of a sledgehammer, making her as jumpy as a kitten. Her legs were so weak that she doubted if she could have moved even had her life depended on it, and she fervently wished she had taken Geoffrey's advice and not come.

It might have been some unconscious betrayal of movement on her part, or some animal instinct of self-preservation in Yusuf's make-up that warned him, she would never know. But the folds of the light screen were flattened together suddenly with a series of sharp clacking sounds, followed immediately by hard fingers closing firmly about Lisa's left arm, and she was jerked out into the open so swiftly that she stumbled and would have fallen if he had not been holding her so tightly.

'Mon dieu!'

He kept his hold on her and it was hard to believe that just for a second or two he was more startled than she was. Lisa got the stunning impression of an overwhelmingly masculine presence, and of grey slacks and a cream shirt that showed the smooth darkness of his body through its texture, and it brought a shivering and uncontrollable response from her senses. Then very deliberately he ran his eyes over her trim figure in white slacks and a pale blue shirt, and Lisa shook her head slowly without having the slightest idea what it was she sought to deny.

'So, Miss Pelham, you have once more managed to force your way in to my presence uninvited!' His arrogance was overwhelming and for the moment Lisa simply looked uncertain, then he released her to take a cigarette and light it. 'Have you no respect at all for the privacy of others?'

Rubbing one hand over the arm he had gripped so tightly, Lisa despaired of him ever seeing her as other than a nuisance. There was a stern, fierce look about his features that discouraged her, and she resented his air of reserve that kept her at arm's length. Most men of her acquaintance were all too ready and willing to flatter and try to please her, but not so this man.

'It was essential that I see you,' she told him, but was irritated by the fact that an unmistakable quaver in her voice gave a quite erroneous impression of meekness. 'I've tried all the conventional ways and failed, so I had to think of some other way.'

'So you chose instead to invade my privacy once more!'

'Would you have seen me if I'd asked for an appointment?' Lisa challenged. 'You know you wouldn't—I've already tried that!'

'But you knew from your—listening in that I would be here today,' he said, and his eyes condemned her for making use of what she had overheard in the restaurant yesterday. 'Tell me, Miss Pelham, do you make a habit of listening to private conversations with the intention of making use of what you hear?'

It was impossible to deny that in this instance she had

done exactly as he said, and the colour in her cheeks confirmed it, but his obvious contempt was very hard to take. She had not expected to feel guilty about what she was doing, and she did not altogether understand her own need to justify herself to him.

'You don't understand how important this is,' she said. 'I don't normally behave like this, but in this instance—well, I just happened to overhear something and took advantage of it because I saw no other way open to me.'

His dark eyes were narrowed, keen and sharp and waiting to pounce, like a cat with a mouse. 'I wonder, Miss Pelham,' he said in a dangerously soft voice, 'if your father is aware of your activities. In his position——'

The unfinished sentence hung like a threat in the air, and Lisa's scalp tingled warningly when she considered its implication. She recalled how interested Yusuf had seemed in the identity of her father, and for the first time it occurred to her that her activities with the group could present a threat to more than Geoffrey's career. Her father's standing with the Moroccan government was very good at the moment, but that unfinished sentence reminded her that this man wielded a great deal of influence, and a complaint about her militant approach could well prove damaging to that good opinion.

'My father knows nothing about this,' she told him, and the very genuine look of anxiety in her eyes must surely have convinced him that she spoke the truth.

But he allowed her to suffer her full share of uncertainty for several moments before he replied. 'I accept that,' he told her eventually. 'I know John Pelham to be an honest and intelligent man, unlikely to condone such behaviour in his daughter if he knew of it.'

'He doesn't even know I belong to the group.' Lisa hastened to strengthen his belief. 'I doubt if he's even heard of Balek!'

'Balek!' He repeated it with such obvious derision that Lisa almost squirmed with embarrassment. 'Is that what all this is about? Is it simply to draw attention to yourself that you tricked your way into my father's house, and now on board the *Djenoun*? Are you so anxious to be noticed, *mademoiselle*, that you resort to any means?'

'No, of course not!'

'Of course not!' He echoed her denial, sweeping his gaze over her flushed and angry face. 'You have no need to resort to such measures, I am sure, Miss Pelham. You must have all the admirers you desire, therefore it is harder for me to imagine the reason for your incredible rashness; for your determination to bring yourself to my notice whether or not I wish to notice you.'

It was not only anger, Lisa realised, that brought the colour to her cheeks and roused the thudding urgency of her pulse to almost deafening force. Obviously he recognised her as more than ordinarily pretty, as most men did, but unlike most men, he made it clear that he was quite unaffected by it, and indeed derided her own awareness of it.

'Please believe me, Mr ben Dacra,' she said, determinedly controlling her voice, 'there is absolutely nothing personal about why I'm here. It's something much more—much more important.'

She no longer sounded meek, and for a second or two she believed she had at least aroused his curiosity. But he was not a patient man, that was obvious, and if she did not come to the point quickly he was quite likely to have her bundled ashore by his crew, having achieved no more than on that first occasion. It was something she could not let happen; not now she had gone to so much trouble to pin him down.

But something was happening that for a moment made her forget all about the group and the warning she had been so intent upon delivering. She stared at him for a second or two, not daring to believe it was true, but forced eventually to accept the fact that, while she had been confronting Yusuf ben Dacra, the crew of his yacht had been going about their routine jobs, quite unaware that they had an extra passenger aboard.

'We're moving!' She turned on him accusingly, in a sudden welter of panic. 'The boat's moving! You must stop it; tell them to turn back!'

His acceptance of the situation unnerved her for a moment, for he drew deeply on the long black Kébir between his lips and narrowed his eyes speculatively behind the drifting smoke from it. 'Of course we are moving, Miss Pelham, I gave the order to sail when I came aboard and my crew have done as I instructed.'

Lisa looked past him to the window that showed tall masts against a cloudless blue sky, sliding slowly past as the *Djenoun* made her way out of Casablanca harbour. Under her feet the carpeted floor vibrated gently with the power of the engines, and to Lisa it was clear that she had been caught in her own trap. She could see little to suggest compassion in the dark features of the man facing her.

'I didn't expect you to sail so soon.'

He must have noticed the slight tremor in her voice, and his eyes gleamed as if with satisfaction. 'I did not expect to find you aboard, *mademoiselle*,' he told her, apparently unconcerned at her plight. 'Not that you could expect me to delay sailing in any case, while you harangued me about some matter that you have so far been very mysterious about.'

Looking around at the sumptuous Arabian Nights setting, Lisa felt curiously unafraid, not at all as she would have expected to feel in such circumstances. She had, after all, got Yusuf ben Dacra's undivided attention for the moment, and she could only take advantage of the situation as she saw it.

'It doesn't matter,' she decided, grasping her opportunity while it was still there, but one look at his face suggested she was being over-optimistic.

'Technically you are a stowaway,' Yusuf informed her with every appearance of being serious. 'I am within my rights to have you put in irons or the equivalent, Miss Pelham. Do not become too sure of yourself—it *does* matter, believe me!'

Lisa eyed him warily. Not so certain now, but not completely deterred either, and looking him in the eye with a confidence she was far from feeling. 'You're on your way to Zobi, aren't you?'

'So much you learned from listening to my conversation,' he reminded her. 'I see no reason to enlighten you further.'

'Because you're ashamed of what you're going to do?'

His eyes narrowed and he looked as if he held his temper only with difficulty. 'I have nothing to be ashamed of,' he informed her in a tight firm voice. 'And I repeat, Miss Pelham, my plans are of no concern to you.'

'They're very much my concern if you insist on destroying Zobi to make way for your wretched hotel!' Lisa insisted in a quick breathless voice; for it was now or never, she realised. 'Your plans are the concern of every right thinking human being when they involve something as callous and ruthless as what you're proposing to do at Zobi!' She warmed to her theme rapidly and her courage rose on a par with her emotional enthusiasm. 'The whole world should know what you mean to do at Zobi!'

She had his attention, she realised a little dizzily, but he was so maddeningly self-controlled, even though his eyes burned fiercely as he watched her. And the fact that he could so successfully contain his emotions when she was so obviously incapable of doing the same, almost made her hate him.

'I have reason to believe that most of the world *does* know about it,' Yusuf remarked coolly. 'Although I doubt whether it has aroused such fervent interest in anyone else. Also,' he went on when she showed signs of continuing her tirade against him, 'I think I should point out that your own situation could quite easily become much less comfortable if you continue in your present vein, Miss Pelham.'

Lisa was shaking like a leaf and it startled her to realise that it was not simply anger that caused it. Somehow crossing swords with this man could be incredibly exciting, no matter how dangerous it might be eventually. 'You don't frighten me, Mr ben Dacra,' she told him. 'I belong to a group of people who care more for humanity than they do for getting rich, and we mean to stop you from destroying Zobi merely to make a profit! If you vandalise those village houses to make way for your luxury hotel, you can expect trouble from us, that's a promise! We've no intention of allowing it!'

'You dare to threaten me?'

'We dare, Mr ben Dacra, because we believe it's important!'

'You are a pack of fools who know nothing about the facts!' His dark eyes glowed blackly and Lisa shivered as they rested immovably on her. 'As for you, *mademoiselle*—you are insolent and hot-headed and I will hear no more of your wild threats! Give me one good reason why I should not have you put into close confinement at this very moment!'

The moist tip of Lisa's tongue flicked anxiously across her lips and she studied his face for a moment from the concealment of her lashes before she replied. 'You wouldn't dare,' she ventured, but she knew even as she said it that Yusuf ben Dacra was a man who would dare anything if he felt himself to be in the right. And for the first time she actually felt afraid of what he might do. 'If anything happens to me——'

Her voice trailed off, and she saw the way his lip curled and the glitter of contempt in his eyes, as if he suspected just how new she was to her role of militant. 'I shall do nothing to you that you cannot have anticipated before you set out on this mission,' he promised. 'But I will not have my privacy constantly threatened by silly young women who have nothing better to do than issue futile warnings. Take my advice, Miss Pelham, and find yourself something less dangerously silly to amuse you in future. Take a lover, he will perhaps teach you that women are made for other things than waving banners.'

'You——'

'That is not so much to your liking?' He interrupted her impatiently, and once more his eyes travelled over her slender form with such explicit interest that she felt herself colouring furiously. 'I am quite sure you would have no difficulty in finding yourself a lover. But in case you came here with the idea of using your not inconsiderable charms to try and persuade me, please do not waste your time or mine. Having been forewarned, I am unlikely to be very easily persuaded!'

It was an unexpected line of attack and Lisa stared at him for a moment, trying to take a firmer grip on her emotions. He must have seen how taken aback she was too, for satisfaction gleamed for a moment in his dark eyes and she hastily avoided them. 'Nothing was further from my mind,' she insisted huskily. 'I can assure you of that!'

'So?' He shrugged carelessly and glanced at his watch. 'I have no more time to waste on you, *mademoiselle*, there are more pressing matters that need my attention.'

'You'll put back to Casablanca so that I can go ashore?'

Until that moment Lisa had had no doubt that was what he would do, but one look at his face was sufficient to tell her how wrong she had been, and she felt her pulse more rapid and urgent suddenly. 'I have no intention of turning back, Miss Pelham, simply to accommodate you. You chose to come aboard without my invitation and you will go ashore when I decide it is convenient for me to *put* you ashore.'

'But you can't keep me here!'

Her plaintive cry followed him to the door of the salon, and he turned slowly to look at her, though it was impossible to read anything into those dark fathomless eyes. His features might have been chiselled from teak, they looked so stern and unrelenting, and Lisa knew there was no hope of persuading him, no matter what means she employed.

'You will find that I can,' he said, and his mouth was set in a firm straight line. 'Not against your will, because you came on board of your own free will and by stealth. I have no doubt that you could contrive to leave again by similar methods, but I would not advise you to try and swim back to Casablanca.'

'Then—what will you do with me?'

It was perhaps tempting fate to have asked him that, and she saw the way he arched his black brows over it. 'Since you have chosen to inflict yourself upon me,' he said, 'you may well be of use eventually. My cook has unfortunately suffered a broken arm and was unable to sail with us this time, so if you prefer the galley to the brig, or a long swim back to Casablanca, you may take his place.'

Lisa stared at him in disbelief. 'You mean you expect me to——'

'I intend to make use of you one way or another,' he interrupted shortly. 'However, I have no time to decide now. I will come back to you when I have attended to other matters.'

He turned swiftly and was gone, closing the door behind him, and leaving Lisa staring dazedly after him. Then, realising how neatly the tables had been turned on her, she pounded angrily on the fat embroidered cushions that furnished the bench seat she sat on. Try as she would, she could see no immediate chance of rescue or escape while they were at sea, and she eventually subsided, curling up among the cushions to gaze disconsolately out of the window.

She had no idea how long she stayed there, looking out at the dazzingly blue sea and at distant passing ships without really seeing them at all, but she realised suddenly that the thudding rhythm of the yacht's engines had changed. Her heart skipped as she sat up straight and listened, catching her breath when the sound stopped altogether. The *Djenoun*, she realised, was no longer moving.

Running to the door, she peered out. The steep companionway was a direct route to the deck, and if the gangway was down and they had not simply come alongside to take on stores, or whatever else Yusuf ben Dacra needed for this trip, she might stand a chance.

Someone walked across the deck, passing across the top of the companionway and she ducked quickly back into the salon. Obviously it was taking a chance going up on deck, and she tried to think of an alternative. The galley, she recalled, was on the other side of the passage, and therefore nearest the shore, and she opened the door of the big kitchen cautiously, heaving a sigh of relief to find it empty.

A window stood half open above a scrubbed work-top and she eyed it eagerly. It could not be a very long drop to the deck from there and she was agile enough to manage it if she was careful not to be seen. She climbed on to the work-top and out through the window with very little trouble, and she crouched below the concealing shadow of the upper deck for a moment or two before venturing a look around to see exactly where she was.

The gods were certainly smiling on her, for she saw that the gangway was only a few metres away and that no one was anywhere near it at the moment. Holding her breath and with her teeth gritted tight, she scuttled along towards it; still crouching low, she made her way down it and scarcely believed her luck when she found herself on a rough stone quay where crates and bundles of skins were stacked high and offered ideal shelter.

She did not stop to wonder where Yusuf ben Dacra might be, but accepted his absence thankfully, only pausing to notice that the crew were occupied with taking aboard what appeared to be a mechanical digger or something similar, its massive bulk carefully protected with sacking to prevent damage to the yacht's beautifully polished deck planking. Lisa doubted very much if she would have remained undetected otherwise.

As it was she was able to slip between the piled crates and decide what her next move should be. She had no idea what the place was, but from the time it had taken them to sail from Casablanca, it could not be too far along the coast, and wherever it was there would almost certainly be a telephone she could use. Her main aim at the moment, however, was to remain unseen until the *Djenoun* departed, and with that in mind, she aimed at getting a little further away from the dock area.

Making her cautious way inland, however, proved less encouraging then she had hoped, and Lisa found to her dismay that the only buildings appeared to be a collection of rather ramshackle warehouses and storage sheds, built in a maze of narrow alleys. She saw no other woman either, as she moved along, only swarthy-faced Moroccans who viewed her arrival in their midst with covert curiosity.

She heard nothing but the throaty sound of Arabic either, and it gave her a curiously lost and alien feeling as she made her way hastily past groups of men who stood haggling together over the piles of cargo. She felt vulnerable too, knowing how she stood out among all those dark faces, with her light hair and fair complexion, and her slim figure quite boldly revealed in slacks and a thin shirt.

It was becoming increasingly evident that every building she saw housed goods rather than people, and it dawned on her gradually that the place, wherever it was, was not a village or a small town as she had first supposed, but purely and simply a remote small port that was used only for commercial transactions. And seldom if ever by Europeans, she guessed.

Not yet actually alarmed by her situation, she wandered about in the various narrow alleys, and they looked so much alike that it was increasingly difficult to recognise whether or not she had been along the same one more than once. Whichever way she turned she seemed to find herself between rows of decrepit warehouses and sheds, until at last she admitted to herself that she was lost.

To make matters worse, the alley she now found herself in appeared to come to a dead end, blocked off by a huge stone shed whose gaping doors tumbled sacking bales out into the alley itself. It smelled between these high walls too, of fish and raw skins, and it buzzed with the inevitable flies, so that she felt her stomach crawl suddenly and put a hand to her mouth as she turned quickly, back the way she had come.

Mouth tightly closed to combat her queasy stomach,

she pulled up short suddenly, her heart thudding hard, when she noticed a man coming along the otherwise deserted alley towards her. He wore the customary long white *djellaba* with the hood drawn up over his head, and the full flowing garment did nothing to impede his stride.

He was a normal enough sight in any Moroccan town or village, yet something about this particular man made her skin prickle warningly, and Lisa watched him uneasily as she took the only way open to her. There was an air of purpose about the tall, striding figure that aroused in her the instinct to run as fast as she could out of his way, and the moment she spotted a narrow opening between two of the buildings she ducked into it, uncaring for the moment where it might take her.

But a swift glance over her shoulder showed that the man was following, turning down the same narrow passageway and hard on her heels, and she took to her heels and ran. Racing breathlessly along the confined space with panic lending speed to her trembling legs, all she could think of was that he had definitely been following her, and she was alarmed in a way she had never been in her life before.

But once again her way was blocked and while she stood breathing hard and shaking like a leaf, with perspiration glistening on her forehead, the man came on purposefully. She dived for the shelter of a half-open doorway, but bales and crates of skins soared before her in an insurmountable pile and she gazed upward hopelessly.

'Oh no!'

Her whispered moan of despair was barely audible even to herself, but she could hear the sound of approaching footsteps above the wild, panicky thudding of her heart. Then, as she spun round defensively, a hand reached out from the snowy folds of the *djellaba* and hard fingers closed around her arm.

Instinctively she struggled, alarmed by the shadowy face so close to her own, but as yet no more than an impression of glittering dark eyes and a mouth set determinedly, and the long brown hands that sought to subdue her. She attempted to hit out, but immediately her arm was released and her hands captured instead and held down in front of her, giving her little option but to look into the face of the man who held her.

'That is enough!' The quiet voice was at once soothing and compelling, and Lisa gazed at Yusuf ben Dacra's face for a moment in disbelief. 'Why are you so frightened? What has happened to you?'

With the glow of panic still in her eyes, Lisa shook her head slowly. In those initial few seconds she had been almost relieved to see him, but now that the panic she had felt was diminishing, it was anger that took over, and she pulled her hands free, shivering with reaction.

'You frightened me half to death,' she accused. Her voice was shaky, and she wondered how her legs were managing to support her when they trembled so. 'I thought you were——'

The accusation trailed off into an uneasy silence under the gaze of those dark eyes. He looked so much at home in the *djellaba* that it was difficult to believe he was other than purely Moroccan, though a quick glance was enough to confirm that he still wore European clothes under it.

It startled her too to realise that in the shadow of the hood his features had a stunningly sensual look that was somehow unexpected, and much too disturbing in the present circumstances. It was inevitable, she thought as she hastily avoided his eyes, that her attempt at escape had been destined to failure from the beginning.

'You were afraid of me?' He asked the question as if the idea of it being true pleased him in some way.

'How could I be expected to recognise you in that?' Lisa demanded, indicating the *djellaba*. 'You've never worn one before.'

'Indeed I have,' Yusuf argued, 'although not on the occasions when you have seen me.' He stood regarding her for a moment with both hands on his hips, speculating on her reaction before he spoke. 'You must realise now what risks you run by walking around a place like this alone,' he said. 'I do not want to have to force you to come back on board the *Djenoun*, *mademoiselle*, but it can be accomplished if you refuse to go with me quietly.'

Lisa was between two stools. This place, wherever it was, seemed to offer little chance of escape back to Casablanca, but on the other hand by returning to the *Djenoun* with Yusuf ben Dacra she was faced with the prospect of becoming ship's cook. At the moment she saw herself with little option, for at least she knew she would have a certain security aboard the yacht. Though she had no intention of giving in without protest.

'You can't *make* me go back with you,' she told him, and tilted her chin in a gesture of defiance that he eyed dubiously.

'Do you imagine I would leave you here, looking as you do?' His eyes raked over her slim shape in slacks and shirt and she remembered how many dark eyes had followed her as she made her way back from the quay. He slid a hand under her arm and curled his strong fingers into her flesh as he urged her forward, out of the shadow of the huge stone shed. 'Come!'

Bitterly disappointed at the failure of her bid to escape him, Lisa felt rather like a captured runaway as they made their way back past the groups of men who still haggled over the goods on the quay. She was aware of the many glances they drew too. Yusuf ben Dacra's tall commanding figure in a flowing white *djellaba*, and herself, small and slender in white slacks and a blue shirt, a captive of the long hard fingers about her arm.

She would have appealed for help, but somehow she knew it would have been useless. Her captor was too impressive, and he was known to them; she was a stranger and a European—an unknown quantity and a potential source of trouble should they interfere. She almost wept with frustration as he ushered her up the gangway once more, and she kept her eyes lowered rather than see the way the crew watched her.

She noticed the window of the galley, now closed after her escape, and the gangway was hauled up almost as soon as they stepped on deck. He let go her arm and sent her ahead of him down the steps, and Lisa tossed back her hair in a final gesture of defiance.

'You'll be sorry for this,' she warned, as he took her back to the big, lushly exotic salon, and Yusuf ben Dacra frowned at her impatiently.

'More threats, Miss Pelham? Do you have no other mood but this most unfeminine one of aggression?' She was thrust down unceremoniously on to one of the seats, and she glared at him defiantly while he pushed back the hood of the *djellaba* and ran his fingers through his black hair. He noticed the flush in her cheeks and the way her hair clung damply to her hot brow, and nodded slowly. 'I will have something cool sent in to you,' he told her. 'You look very hot.'

'I don't *want* anything, thank you!'

Yusuf said nothing for a moment, although his eyes showed such contempt for her churlishness that Lisa felt a curl of embarrassment and hastily lowered her eyes. 'You refuse something cool to drink, simply to make a point?' His voice was as scathing as the look in his eyes. 'That is very foolish of you, *mademoiselle*, but the choice is yours.' His lips tightened and he was already half-turned to go. 'You will remain here until we are safely out of port, and then you may go wherever you wish, as long as you do not hinder the crew.'

Sitting disconsolately on one of the bench seats along under the window, Lisa felt suddenly very small and lost as she watched his tall angry figure go striding across the room, and she swallowed her pride and called after him rather than let him simply abandon her to her own devices.

'Mr ben Dacra!' He turned, his head back and looking at her down the length of his arrogant nose. Politeness was inbred in him too deeply for him to ignore an obvious plea, but he was grudging in his courtesy, and Lisa used her hands in a fluttering gesture of apology and pleading. 'I'm sorry—I would appreciate a drink, thank you.'

At least he did not show even a hint of satisfaction that she had climbed down, but merely raised one brow a fraction. 'Have you a preference?'

Lisa shook her head. 'No. No, just anything will do—thank you.'

He inclined his head briefly. 'I will see to it.'

He turned and was gone, leaving Lisa staring at the firmly closed door and wondering if she could possibly be dreaming all this. It was obviously not going to be easy getting away from him, and yet she could not bring herself to abandon the idea of trying.

She had delivered the message she had been entrusted with and there was no more she could do in that direction, but she felt the need to get away from Yusuf ben Dacra as soon as she possibly could. Much as she hated to admit it, she found him much too attractive to make it wise to stay in too close contact with him. Knowing how he felt about her made it impossible to think along those lines.

Lisa felt cool and refreshed, and she was once more

prowling about the salon, restless and uneasy, yet uncertain what she could do about her present predicament. From now on it was certain that her movements would be much more closely watched, and she wondered, not entirely without a sense of anticipation, just how long Yusuf ben Dacra meant to keep her aboard.

If she did not arrive home before morning, Madame Raymond, their housekeeper, would be alarmed, and if she told Geoffrey, as she most likely would in the first place, he would know at once where Lisa was. Inevitably, if Geoffrey believed her to be trapped aboard the *Djenoun*, he would alert her father, and at this stage she did not want her father involved. It was all so very much in the air at the moment, but she almost wished for nightfall so that the ball would start rolling that would free her; for she felt sure he would not detain her overnight.

She was kneeling on the bench below one of the windows, watching the azure sky, cloudless and hazed with gold, when the door opened and Yusuf returned. Lisa watched him anxiously, then realised that he must recognise her anxiety, and immediately took steps to change the impression.

Brushing back her hair, she sat with one leg curled up under her, long lashes concealing what was in her eyes. 'Well?' she said with as much aplomb as she could summon. 'When do I go home?'

He had dispensed with the *djellaba* and looked rather less over-aweing in European clothes; though only a little less so. He had probably been on deck, she guessed, watching him from below her lashes, because he had a warm, fresh, sea smell about him, and his dark face glowed with the heat of the sun.

The cream shirt clung even more tightly to his body with the dampness of physical exertion, and he brushed a careless hand through the hair at his brow as he came across the salon towards her. He was a very disturbing man, but she hated herself for admitting it, and took the trouble to avoid his eyes.

'If you will come with me, Miss Pelham.'

It was more of a command than a request and Lisa's chin automatically thrust out in defiance. She did not get up, but sat looking at him, her reaction in no doubt. 'Where to?' she demanded.

'First to the cabin you have been allocated and then to see the galley where you will be taking over from Hassan.'

Lisa's eyes gleaming defiance. 'I have no intention of signing on as your cook,' she told him, clinging with both hands to the edge of the seat. 'I demand to be put ashore!'

'You *demand?*' He came closer and Lisa shivered quite involuntarily. From the shadow of thick black lashes his eyes surveyed her steadily. 'You are in no position to demand, Miss Pelham. I am giving you the choice of helping in the galley or of being locked in your cabin; the choice is yours.'

'You have no right——' Lisa began, but was cut short with harsh impatience.

'I have every right to put you under lock and key, *mademoiselle,*' he informed her with chilling confidence. 'You came aboard my vessel uninvited and by stealth, and you have threatened me with violence if I do not meet your demands concerning a scheme to improve the amenities of my country. I have every right to treat you as a felon, and to hand you over to the authorities the moment we touch land again! Do not presume to tell me my rights, *mademoiselle,* I am well aware of them, and you would find the authorities much less lenient than I am, should you force my hand!'

Lisa stopped to consider what would happen if he did hand her over to the police, as he was entitled to, she knew. She could imagine how her father would feel; how embarrassed he would be by her arrest as a militant protester, but she could not find it in her heart to abandon the group or the project at this late stage. Instead she would have to tread more carefully, think before she took another step, and she shifted uneasily on the seat, looking down at her hands rather than at Yusuf.

'How do you know I can cook?' she asked, and he laughed shortly.

'If you cannot,' he said, 'it will be no more than I expect of you, for you seem to be singularly lacking in the normal feminine virtues!'

Lisa flushed angrily and got up from the seat, her eyes gleaming angrily at him. Never before had a man been so determinedly unaffected by her as a woman, and she found the experience not only bad for her morale, but challenging too. Though she did not yet recognise the danger of that situation.

'No one else has ever complained about me being unfeminine,' she informed him, and her voice shivered resentfully. 'Perhaps you're not a very good judge, Mr ben Dacra!'

Yusuf eyed her slowly and with great deliberation, from head to toe, his dark gaze lingering appraisingly on every soft curve, until Lisa felt that the pale blue shirt and white slacks had been stripped from her. 'No doubt if I had a taste for sun-bleached hair and pink cheeks I would find you attractive enough,' he observed dispassionately. 'In any event I have no time to pander to your ego, Miss Pelham. Will you help willingly, or must I lock you in your cabin until we land, then hand you over to the police to deal with?'

It was blackmail, pure and simple, Lisa recognised, but there was little she could do against it. She had done quite enough to make a charge of stowing away and offering a threat stick in any court of law, and she had to think of her father, however belatedly. For the moment she could do nothing but go along with it, and she shrugged resignedly.

'I'll help,' she said.

He nodded, but when she saw the gleam of satisfaction in his eyes, Lisa clenched her hands tightly, itching to hit out at him. He had it far too much his own way at the moment, but her time would come. 'First I will show you to your cabin,' he told her; just as if she was an invited guest, Lisa thought a little wildly as she followed him along the passageway.

She noticed how his broad shoulders almost filled the width of the passage, and the fact that his head almost brushed the low ceiling, so that he walked with it slightly bowed. His footsteps whispered softly over the glossy linoleum, and she saw that he had exchanged his ordinary shoes for a pair of *babouches* in light-coloured leather.

About halfway along the passage he stopped and opened a door, indicating with a brief inclination of his head that she should enter the cabin he had allotted her. When he followed her in he had to duck his head slightly, she noted, through the low doorway, and once inside he dominated the small cabin.

Lisa looked around, hoping to criticise, but she could find no fault with it. Shiny wood panels in some pale shade similar to pine covered the walls, and the single bed was covered with a richly embroidered coverlet. The one window looked out over the open sea, and air-conditioning kept the atmosphere pleasantly cool, while carpet deadened their footsteps as they walked in.

She liked it, though she was not prepared to admit it, and she also felt a stirring of excitement that she could not quite account for. It was not as if she was there to enjoy herself; until Yusuf ben Dacra allowed her ashore, she was virtually a prisoner, and expected to work as well.

'There's a key to this door?'

She asked the question impulsively, and his black brows arched swiftly as, thumbs hooked in the waist of his slacks, he stood watching her. 'There is a key,' he agreed, and Lisa's brain worked swiftly, though not along the lines he suspected, evidently. 'But you have no need to fear an invasion of your privacy, *mademoiselle*; none of my men will come near you, I give you my word on it.' Briefly he managed to hold her evasive gaze, and she saw the deep gleaming challenge in their depths before she looked away. 'And you have my word that you are safe from my attentions.'

The colour high in her cheeks, Lisa looked up at him. 'I'm quite aware of your opinion of me, Mr ben Dacra,' she said, as coolly as she was able in the circumstances, 'but I'll lock my door just the same!'

'As you wish!' He turned and was already in the doorway when something else seemed to come to him and he about-turned to face her once more. His eyes, she noticed, were narrowed and vaguely suspicious. 'If you should have any idea of locking yourself in your cabin as a way of avoiding your kitchen duties, Miss Pelham,' he told her, 'I would not advise it.'

Lisa blinked at him, piqued because he had apparently found her so easy to comprehend. 'If I did, at least I shouldn't have to work in your wretched galley,' she said peevishly, and Yusuf regarded her for a second or two in silence, as if he seriously considered the possibility of her doing it.

'That might be true,' he allowed in a quiet matter-of-fact voice after a moment or two, 'but then neither would you eat. So think carefully before you do anything rash, Miss Pelham.'

Lisa stared at him, much too uncertain that she knew

him well enough to risk it. 'You can't *do* this to me,' she insisted, though with no degree of confidence, and Yusuf ben Dacra eyed her with his steady dark eyes for a moment.

'Do not doubt that I can, *mademoiselle,*' he assured her confidently, and Lisa watched the door close firmly behind him, almost expecting to hear the sound of a key turning in the lock; breathing deeply in relief when it did not happen.

Yusuf ben Dacra was every bit as ruthless and unpredictable as she had feared, and she wished she knew just how many chances she could take without incurring some terrible vengeance. He was very much an unknown quantity, especially as far as his private life was concerned, and she saw him not only as a disturbingly attractive man, but a potentially dangerous one as well. In the circumstances she could not understand her own behaviour at all, and she sighed inwardly in despair as she opened the door and went in search of the galley.

CHAPTER FOUR

LISA had done quite a bit of cooking at various times, and Madame Raymond had even initiated her into some of the mysteries of the Moroccan menu, which the crew of the *Djenoun* would be sure to expect. But she was far from expert, and she approached her first attempt at feeding a crew of hungrey men with mingled alarm and defiance.

Fortunately the yacht boasted a freezer, well stocked with chickens, mutton and beef, and there were plenty of vegetables. But she would have been happier cooking a roast and two vegetables, the kind of meal an English crew would have enjoyed. Eventually she settled for making a *tajin*, which was the Moroccan equivalent of a stew, but much more exotic.

The ingredients, she knew, included chickens and vegetables and spices, but she was completely in the dark about such things as quantities and cooking times, so she had to trust her own judgment. In the event she put in a lavish amount of everything, since Madame Raymond had assured her that that was an important factor in Moroccan cooking, and hoped for the best.

If her efforts were successful and the crew enjoyed what she cooked, then well and good, but if not, then the idea lurked at the back of her mind that a disastrous first attempt could mean that Yusuf ben Dacra might have second thoughts. She had little hope of pleasing his personal tastes, she told herself. She even toyed with the idea of deliberately making it a disaster, but decided against it eventually.

The finished result looked fairly edible when she sent

it out in two big terracotta dishes, but she did not venture to sample it herself. Having cooked it she had no appetite left and instead of eating she went up on deck in the air. It was hot outside, but at least the air was fresh and not heavy with the odours of cooking, and she breathed it in thankfully.

Apart from herself, the only other person around as far as she could see, was a young man at the wheel, and from the brief, almost sly look he gave her Lisa guessed Yusuf ben Dacra had been telling the truth when he guaranteed that none of his men would trouble her. In a way she was sorry, for since she came aboard the *Djenoun* that morning she had spoken with no one but her determined jailer, and conversation with someone else would have done a lot to relieve her feelings.

But whatever she felt, it was impossible not to experience something of the pleasure and excitement that being on the water always gave her. The sky was a clear cobalt blue hazed with gold, and the sea itself shimmered darkly like the sinuous softness of silk as it rippled away from the *Djenoun*'s leisurely progress.

The yacht itself was beautiful too, just as Yusuf had claimed, and Lisa could well understand his pride and pleasure in her. His yacht, she thought ruefully, was probably the only thing he truly loved, and he had declared that even she was hard to handle at times. Even from those he loved, he expected obedience.

She spotted a couple of other boats, sketched in shadowy outline against the sky and sea, and thought that they were probably making for Casablanca. Watching them she felt restless with frustration, for both were too far away for her to make any attempt to attract attention, and she guessed Yusuf ben Dacra had taken that fact into account too.

Moving around to the landward side of the yacht the prospect was no more encouraging at the moment. Ragged cliffs tumbled down to the sea like granite waterfalls, and looked so grimly forbidding that Lisa turned from them, frowning. She dared not dwell on how long she was likely to be aboard, but the longer she was there, the more desperate she became. And when she returned to her own cabin a short time later, she flung herself down on the bed and stared at the ceiling in angry frustration.

It was possible, she supposed, that some women would find it exciting being the virtual prisoner of a man like Yusuf ben Dacra, but to Lisa the fact was becoming more and more worrying. He must surely let her go before nightfall, if they touched land again. He might be planning to put her ashore and then continue down to Zobi, thinking he had damped her enthusiasm for the group and their cause.

A light tap on her door made her sit up suddenly and catch her breath, and she was appalled to realise that the thudding beat of her heart was because she expected Yusuf ben Dacra to be out there. Apparently her lack of response called for more demanding measures, for another knock, louder and more insistent, followed almost immediately and she slid off the bed to answer it.

Lisa had been expecting to see Yusuf and when it turned out not to be him, but a young man in a white cotton jacket who eyed her curiously, she blinked in surprise. Then he smiled, a quick appreciative gleam in his dark eyes that suggested that either he had not been informed of Yusuf's ruling concerning her, or that he chose to ignore it. Two rows of crooked but stunningly white teeth showed in his handsome brown face and he leaned slightly towards her eagerly.

'*Mademoiselle*; Monsieur ben Dacra requests that you join him if you please.'

His English was good but very strongly accented, and for a second or two Lisa gazed at him uncomprehendingly. It was natural for her to suspect Yusuf ben Dacra's motives, whatever he did, and this summons was so completely unexpected that she looked for an ulterior motive as a matter of course.

'Mademoiselle?'

She was prodded gently back to realisation, and she attempted a smile, still standing in the door of her cabin. 'Why does Mr ben Dacra want to see me?' she asked, and the young man looked briefly puzzled.

But seemingly he had been entrusted with the task of taking her to his employer, and he was anxious to carry it out. 'Please will you come, *mademoiselle?*' he coaxed, his crooked smile beaming persuasively. 'Monsieur ben Dacra is waiting.'

'Not until I know *why* he wants to see me,' Lisa insisted, not moving an inch.

'Why, to eat luncheon in *la salle à manger*, of course, *mademoiselle.*' From his expression she thought he found her rather slow for not realising it. 'You will come now?'

But to Lisa enlightenment merely brought a new dilemma. She had never expected anything as civilised as an invitation to lunch, and she still looked for an ulterior motive. 'You mean he expects—he wants me to have lunch with him?'

The young man nodded, plainly puzzled by her reticence, and it was in Lisa's mind to refuse out of hand to sit down to a meal with her tyrannical host. But by now she was beginning to feel hungry and the invitation was far more tempting than it would have been an hour earlier. Her empty stomach clamoured for food and Yusuf ben Dacra was offering her lunch, even if it was her own *tajin*. There was only one way she could reply, though she did so with obvious reluctance.

'Very well,' she said, 'I'll come. Though I look as bedraggled as a gypsy, after hours in that wretched kitchen.'

'Mademoiselle?'

In no mood to explain, Lisa dismissed his encouraging smile with a shake of her head, then followed him out into the passageway and as far as a door at the far end, next to the galley. Heaven knew what had prompted the invitation, but a suspicion that it was primarily to complain about her cooking was firmly implanted by the time she was ushered into the dining salon, and she was already frowning defensively.

Yusuf was standing by a window at the far end, but he turned the moment she came in, and once more Lisa was struck by the sheer animal magnetism of the man. He surveyed her boldly, arrogantly, his gaze sweeping over her flushed face in frank appraisal before he spoke, and taking in every detail of her dishevelled hair and the way the blue shirt clung to her body because she was still hot and sticky, even after a spell on deck.

'Please come in, Miss Pelham.'

His cool and matter-of-fact reception of her was an added irritation to Lisa, for he sounded as if he was welcoming an invited and honoured guest, instead of someone who he knew would give him the slip at the very first opportunity. Rather than respond in the same way, she studiously ignored him for the moment and instead took deliberate stock of her surroundings while he stood watching her.

Yusuf ben Dacra certainly believed in his comfort, even on the high seas, for the salon, although simple in comparison, was no less comfortable than the big, palatial one amidships. A long highly polished table ran the whole width of it and took up most of the space, although there was seating room for about a dozen people, Lisa guessed.

At the moment it was set for only two, with gleaming silver and snowy white linen, crystal wine glasses glinting like diamonds in the diffused sunlight coming in through the window. Briefly Lisa thanked heaven she was not expected to eat Moroccan style with her fingers, for she had never yet acquired the necessary skill it required to eat a meal without getting into an embarrassing mess.

The floor was carpeted, the rich traditional Rabat carpet, like in the big salon, and the walls were white; plain white except for a light stippling of gold that added richness without being garish. It was unusual to see pictures on the walls of a Moroccan home, even a floating one, but two rather good pen and ink drawings hung on the wall at the window end, and Lisa noted them with interest.

One subject she could identify without any trouble. It was very definitely Sheik Abhan el Boudri, Yusuf's adopted father, but the man in the other drawing intrigued her more because she suspected he might be Yusuf's natural father, Joseph d'Acra. She wasn't quite sure why she thought it might be Joseph d'Acra, but the man was obviously European. About thirty years old, she guessed, younger than Yusuf was now, but with something basically similar in the angle of the head and the cast of the features, but fair instead of dark.

Both places had been set at the same end of the table; one at the head and the other to the right of it, and just for a second Lisa felt an insane desire to giggle at the thought of her amateurishly contrived *tajin* being served in such luxurious surroundings. It was much more than it deserved, as her host would soon find out.

Turning her attention to him at last, she found him still watching her with that unwavering gaze, and it was irresistible to angle her chin the way she did, and to meet his eyes with her own dark and resentful blue ones. 'You'll have to make allowances for the way I look,' she told him in an aggressively husky voice. 'I've been working in the kitchen for hours and it's very hot and sticky. As you'll know, I've nothing I can change into.'

'That is something that will be remedied,' he told her, in such a quietly confident voice that Lisa looked up sharply at him, for it suggested that her stay was likely to be long enough for her to need a change of clothes.

'I shouldn't need any more clothes, if I——'

'Please sit down, Miss Pelham.' He interrupted her, smoothly cutting across her protest as if she had not made it, and for a moment Lisa felt herself trembling with annoyance.

But he had drawn out the chair next to his own at the head of the table and there was little point in refusing to sit and eat with him now that she had come this far. Her eyes when she looked at him were wary and defiant, and she was far more anxious than she had any intention of letting him know.

'I'd like to know just how long you intend keeping me here against my will,' she said, doing her best to steady her voice.

Still standing with his hands on the back of the chair he had pulled out for her, Yusuf regarded her for a moment in silence, his dark eyes disturbingly confident. 'You will remain for as long as it is necessary,' he informed her. 'Now will you please sit down and eat some lunch, Miss Pelham, I am sure you must be hungry.'

She could not deny it and, since there seemed little chance of anything else coming her way, Lisa did as he said and sat down. Unwelcome guest or not, she was treated with courtesy, she noted when her chair was pulled out for her. And yet again, when he leaned over her, she was made aware of his vibrant masculinity.

His brown hands hovered for a moment while she settled into her seat, and powerful-looking arms reminded her of how she had once been carried in them to the comfort of his car. An open neck revealed a vee of brown throat and through a soft cream shirt the warmth of his body touched her for a moment, bringing havoc to her heartbeat. She had never in her life been so affected by the sheer sensual virility of a man, and she sighed in almost audible relief when he moved away to take his own seat.

'I hope the food is to your taste,' he said when he was seated, and Lisa looked at him curiously.

'You mean the *tajin* I made?' she asked. 'I can't guarantee it, I've never attempted it before and I had to guess at the recipe.'

Yusuf eyed her in a way that stirred up those ever-present suspicions again. 'I hope you were successful,' he told her. 'Both for the sake of my crew and for your sake. But you will not be eating the *tajin*; Ali prepares my meals separately. Ali is my personal servant,' he added, as if it was essential that he explain, and looked up for a moment when the same young man who had summoned her to lunch, put in another appearance. 'I hope he has chosen something you will like.'

Lisa had to admit to a sense of relief when she learned he would not after all be eating the *tajin*, for she felt certain he would have found something to criticise. In fact she was so hungry herself now, that she would have eaten anything that the smiling Ali provided. 'Whatever it is, I shall like it,' she assured him. 'I'm so hungry, and it seems like hours since I had breakfast.'

'You were about early, of course.' The smooth deep polite voice almost sounded as if he sympathised with her, although she found it hard to believe it. 'Please eat as much as you like, I am sure Ali has prepared plenty.'

Ali responded with a wide, crooked smile as he brought in their lunch. He was well trained; his slight figure moved back and forth between them, swiftly and fairly unobtrusively, serving dishes of cold chicken and salad, and beaming encouragingly whenever he managed to catch Lisa's eye.

He was seemingly under the impression that she

needed encouragement, and Lisa wondered just how much he knew about her situation. She speculated on the likelihood of his being willing to help her, should she make another attempt to leave the *Djenoun*, but second thoughts suggested that he was probably unlikely to go that far in his sympathy, and risk angering his employer.

Yusuf poured the wine himself; a light French one that Lisa found very pleasant but rather more potent than she anticipated when she drank the first glass of it on a virtually empty stomach. Very little was said and, as Ali left the room, he caught her eye once more, giving her the merest suggestion of a wink and another of his beaming smiles. It was automatic to glance at Yusuf ben Dacra to see if he had noticed and quite unexpected when she realised he was already looking at her.

'I didn't expect this,' she confessed when his black brows arched curiously, and he frowned.

'You did not expect to be given a meal?' he asked. 'But my promise was that if you did not do as I asked and work in the galley you would not eat, *mademoiselle*. You *have* done as I said, so of course you have a meal yourself.'

Lisa's eyes challenged him from the shadow of her lashes. 'And if I hadn't?'

He did not answer at once and it was impossible to read what was in his eyes. 'Then I would have had to see how long you could stand being hungry, Miss Pelham. I feel sure you would have yielded before you reached starvation!'

Uncomfortably suspicious that he meant exactly what he said, Lisa gave her attention once more to her meal, doing her best to ignore a wildly thudding heartbeat that she suspected had more to do with excitement than fear of that dark threatening face opposite. 'What I meant was that I didn't expect the honour of sitting at the captain's table,' she told him, quite unrepentant about the hint of sarcasm. Just briefly she caught his eye, challenging him to explain the unexpected gesture. 'I thought the galley or the crew's quarters would be my lot in the circumstances. It's what your usual cook would get, isn't it?'

Yusuf sampled another mouthful of chicken before he answered her, and for the moment his eyes were hidden by the thickness of his lashes. Lisa suspected he knew just how curious she was about his invitation, but whether or not he was prepared to satisfy her curiosity remained to be seen.

'You are, I believe, intelligent enough to know that I cannot treat you in exactly the same way as I would Hassan,' he said.

'Of course,' Lisa agreed with deception meekness. 'You couldn't drive Hassan with the threat of starvation, could you?'

Ignoring the attempt to make him angry, Yusuf shifted his dark gaze slowly over her features and came to rest on her mouth with a lingering intensity that made her shiver. 'Neither do I believe you are under any delusion concerning your more obvious attractions, *mademoiselle*, although you will find most Moroccan men rather less easy to seduce than the type you are probably accustomed to. I keep you separate from my crew, Miss Pelham, more for their sake than for yours.'

Lisa's heart was beating so urgently that she found it hard to swallow the morsel of chicken she had in her mouth before she answered him. Then raising her chin slightly, she met his eyes for just a moment. 'It may surprise you to learn that I hadn't even thought of seducing your crew,' she told him in a slightly choked voice. 'You seem to have a curious idea of my morals, Mr ben Dacra. And if you really don't like having me aboard, the remedy is in your own hands. Put me ashore and you have no more worries about me corrupting your men, or of having to answer charges of abduction!'

'Abduction?' His dark eyes regarded her steadily and something she saw in them made her uneasy without her being quite sure why. It was a certain air of confidence, over and above his normal arrogance. 'The question of your being abducted does not arise, *mademoiselle*, not when it is known that you came aboard the *Djenoun* of your own free will.'

'Not the second time!'

His eyes glittered darkly at her, unmoved by her faint threat. 'No man would have left you at Bouli on your own,' he told her. 'I would have been guilty of extreme callousness if I had abandoned you in such a place, and your father would have had every right to blame me for whatever happened to you!'

Reminding her of her father brought a momentary twinge of longing for him, but it was a moment she hastily dismissed. She could take care of herself, she had told her father as much when she came to Morocco, and she believed she could, no matter what her present circumstances were.

'If I don't arrive home,' she began, but fell silent when he shook his head.

'You have gone to spend a few days with a friend,' said Yusuf, using his hands to emphasise the point. 'Young women are seldom if ever abducted by romantic sheiks in this liberated age, Miss Pelham; it is so unlikely that no one would believe it!'

'I wasn't thinking of you——'

Her voice trailed off when he said something in French. She did not understand it, but something in his voice and the gleaming darkness of his eyes brought a swift flush of colour to her cheeks. Hastily she looked away, trying to keep her voice steady.

'You wouldn't approve of the liberated woman, of course,' she said.

Yusuf raised a brow and got on with his meal. 'I am no woman-hater,' he assured her quietly, 'but I confess that my tastes tend more towards the less aggressive type of female.'

Looking down into her wine glass Lisa tilted it round and round, watching the contents spin and whirl like liquid gold in the light. 'You don't believe in freedom.' She said it without for a moment really believing it, despite what she knew about him. And Yusuf confirmed it by shaking his head firmly, as if he had complete confidence in his own argument.

'Of course I believe in freedom,' he said. 'What I cannot agree with is the complete reversal of roles where men and women are concerned. History and evolution have shown that women do not naturally take to the dominant role, nor do they need to with so many alternative means of influence at their disposal. I do not grudge women their liberty, *mademoiselle*, in some spheres it is long overdue, but I cannot see the advantage of living in a society where they dominate at the expense of their femininity.' His eyes regarded her with such intensity that Lisa was bound to look at him. 'I am more easily persuaded than threatened, Miss Pelham, like most of my kind.'

Such an obvious allusion to her own attitude was impossible to mistake, and Lisa felt a curious tingle of excitement as she listened to him, even though she did not agree with his theories. Putting her glass to her lips she eyed him with deliberate provocation over its rim while she spoke.

'Like most of your kind, you have no doubt at all that men have the upper hand by some God-given right, do you?' she challenged, and it was typical of him, Lisa thought, that he did not attempt to deny it.

'I would rather cosset a woman than have to regard her in the same light as I would another man,' he said. 'I am not given to dealing gently with an aggressive opponent, no matter who it might be. Yes, *mademoiselle*, you are right; in the man-woman relationship I like to think I have the dominant role, and I believe that is the way a lot of women like it too.'

'I see.' Sitting there with the wine glass between her hands, Lisa appeared suitably submissive, but when she looked up suddenly, he could hardly have missed the bright gleam in her eyes. 'You sound very confident, Mr ben Dacra. But I would scarcely call it cosseting a woman to force her into a menial post that she has no talent for, and hasn't the slightest inclination for. Nor would I call it cosseting her to hold her against her will on a yacht crewed entirely by men.'

Yusuf's eyes condemned her dramatic summing up, and it was futile to think she was going to be allowed to get away with it. 'And I would remind you, Miss Pelham, that your present situation was brought about entirely by your own actions. You came aboard the *Djenoun* uninvited, and threatened me with violence; you are very lucky to be getting off so lightly. As for the rest, I have given you my word that no man on board will lay a hand on you.'

'And you count yourself a man too?'

Lisa felt curiously lightheaded, filled with a wild, inexplicable chaos of emotions that made her heart beat hard and fast. But she was already regretting her impulsiveness, for not only had she been indefensibly rude, she had destroyed whatever frail chance of a truce had existed during the last few minutes.

Yusuf's mouth tightened ominously and the knuckles of his fingers showed starkly white through the tanned skin as he gripped the stem of his glass. 'If I found aggressive viragos to my liking,' he said harshly, 'you would have discovered before now whether or not I am a man, *mademoiselle*!'

Appalled at the fury she had aroused, Lisa shook her head in an attempt to mollify him. 'I—I didn't mean——'

Roughly he cut her short. 'Give me credit for a little intelligence, *mademoiselle*! I know exactly what you meant, and I hope that you have now salvaged your pride with that minor victory!'

Lisa was alarmed to realise how close to tears she was, and she could not imagine why. As Yusuf said, she should feel satisfied with her minor victory, but instead she regretted even having thought of taking such a petty revenge. 'Please,' she ventured, 'I really didn't mean that the way it sounded.'

'Oh, but I think you did, Miss Pelham,' he declared confidently. 'You reacted in what I can only assume is your customary style, and I should have been prepared for something of the sort.' He placed his knife and fork carefully side by side on his empty plate, and spoke without looking at her. 'If you have finished,' he went on in the same cool hard voice, 'I will call Ali to serve the second course. But please do me the favour of remaining silent so that I may enjoy the rest of my meal without losing my temper.'

Trembling and unhappy, and scarcely knowing who to blame for the way she felt, Lisa got swiftly to her feet; almost stumbling when the chair legs caught in the carpet and impeded her turn. 'Please don't bother for me,' she said huskily, 'I've had enough. If you'll excuse me, I'll go back to my cabin.'

It was unfamiliar and rather alarming to feel as horribly vulnerable as she did at the moment, and Lisa wished Geoffrey could have been there to reassure her. It seemed such an interminable distance to the door that she could not imagine how he managed to get there before her. His big hands behind him against the wood panels in a seemingly casual stance, he stood blocking her way, and Lisa dared not raise her eyes any higher than the set sternness of his mouth for the moment.

'Please sit down and finish your lunch,' he said firmly. 'There is no need to aggravate the situation any further by making a martyr of yourself, Miss Pelham. Your friends will not thank you for it.'

'My friends?' Lisa stared at him for a second uncomprehendingly, then shook her head slowly. It was incredible to think that, just for a moment, she had forgotten why she was there. 'You're wrong if you think I was trying to be a martyr,' she told him in a small shaky voice that was unlikely to convince anybody, and particularly Yusuf ben Dacra. 'I'm simply not hungry any more, that's all.'

The touch of his hand under her chin was unexpected and caught her unawares so that she gasped aloud, looking up swiftly with wide, wary eyes. For a moment he stood looking down into her face with his customary boldness, taking explicit note of every single feature, including the flush on her cheeks and the fact that she soon lowered her eyes again.

'You are an incredibly bad liar,' he stated firmly and with unexpected frankness. His long fingers spread out over her face, cupping her chin in his palm. 'If you are to work, you must eat, and I must remind you that you have another meal to provide for the crew this evening.'

'Oh, I *can't*!'

For a moment she believed she shook him with the fierceness of her protest, but his surprise was short-lived and his dark eyes gleamed a warning. 'You have proved that you can,' he insisted. 'And do you not have a saying in England, that practice makes perfect? It is very true, you will find.'

It wasn't merely anger that made her tremble so, Lisa realised. She felt alarmingly helpless and very close to tears as she stood there facing him. He would probably have revelled in the idea of making her weep, even in sheer frustration, but he was unlikely to be moved by tears now. Her stock was much too low at the moment. Just the same her voice had a shiveringly husky sound and her eyes were just a little too bright.

'You can't go keeping me here,' she told him shakily. 'It—it just isn't right!'

'Right?' She had not realised that he still had his hand beneath her chin, and his fingers closed a little more tightly for a moment, curving into her cheek. 'By what right did you bring yourself aboard my vessel, eh? By what right did you invade my privacy and threaten me with your silly warnings? You talk of right, *mademoiselle*, as if you alone are entitled to have rights!'

Lisa's mouth trembled, there was nothing she could do to stop it. She wanted to beg him to let her go home, but she was prevented from doing so by the last shreds of her pride. She would not beg him for her freedom, but something in her eyes made the appeal silently when she raised her eyes to him.

'You're every bit as hard and unfeeling as I expected you to be,' she accused huskily. 'You're an arrogant, selfish monster and I wish I'd never come on board your wretched yacht!'

His mouth tightened into a hard straight line and she caught her breath audibly when he gripped her by her upper arms and pulled her close to the lean hardness of his body. 'So do I,' he murmured between gritted teeth. '*Mon dieu*, so do I!'

Lisa offered no resistance because the move took her by surprise, and a swift upward glance showed his eyes gleaming darkly in the second before he bent his head and the warm, spicy touch of his mouth parted her lips, bruising in its hardness. Alarming and exciting and breathtaking in its fierceness.

It was a deliberate assault on her senses that left her without strength or resistance, and tremblingly limp and pliant in his arms. When he let her go the strong, bruising fingers slid from her arms slowly, almost reluctantly, and she took a moment or two to recover her breath, looking up at him with blank, stunned eyes.

He turned away quickly and walked back to the table, standing with his back to the light and one hand running through his hair. It was impossible to judge his feelings from what she could see of his face, but that gesture with his hand through his hair seemed to suggest he was less perfectly composed than his voice implied.

'You are doubtless familiar with this kind of situation,' he said, and quite incredibly seemed to believe it. 'But it is something I had not meant to happen, and I am sorry that I allowed it to.'

Lisa stared at him, finding it hard to believe that he really was more concerned with his own lack of self-control than with the effect he had had on her emotions; and she hated him for a moment for judging her so inaccurately. She had never before been so affected by a single kiss, and yet he seemed quite unaware of how he had shaken her.

The back of one hand to her lips, Lisa stared across at him for a moment or two, then shook her head slowly. 'Do you honestly believe I take that sort of thing in my stride?' she demanded huskily. 'Do you see me as promiscuous as well as—as militant and—and all the other unfeminine vices you attribute to me?'

Her reproach seemed to puzzle him, for he was frowning slightly and his dark eyes looked curious. 'I cannot believe you have never been kissed before,' he said, and she noticed that his own voice was deep and husky. 'You are not so inexperienced, surely.'

Lisa tried to think of some way to tell him the truth. But how would he understand that the brief, light caresses that so often followed an evening out bore no resemblance at all to the violent assault on her emotions that he had just subjected her to? So instead of trying to explain, she turned and opened the door.

'You wouldn't believe me if I told you the truth,' she said in a small and very unsteady voice.

But as she turned to close the door behind her, she glanced across at the tall, lean figure standing with his back to the window, and her heart quickened urgently in response to the look she saw in his eyes. A deep glowing darkness that was almost as affecting as the burning fierceness of his mouth had been.

'Oh, but I think that perhaps I might, *ma chère mademoiselle*,' he told her softly. And Lisa quickly closed the door against the smile that touched his mouth with such sensual warmth it made her heart turn over.

CHAPTER FIVE

LISA was still trying to decide what to make for the evening meal when Ali poked his head around the galley door, and it was automatic to smile in response to his white-toothed beam. Encouraged by her smile, he came across and stood beside her while she went on preparing vegetables, although she did not know what she would do with them yet.

Almost certainly, she thought, Ali would be included with the rest of the crew in the ban on fraternisation, so she assumed he was there on Yusuf's instructions. It was that made her eye him suspiciously after her initial greeting. 'Are you here to make sure I do my job properly?' she asked. 'Or wasn't the *tajin* up to the standard expected on the *Djenoun?*'

Ali's grimace could have meant anything, but he laughed a second later, his eyes twinkling good-naturedly. 'The *tajin* was very good for a——'

'Were you going to say a foreigner or an amateur?' Lisa guessed ruefully. 'I don't mind you being honest about it, Ali, but I hope the crew blame their boss if they don't like what they get. I didn't ask for the job!'

'Monsieur ben Dacra has said that I should help for a little time,' Ali told her, and was seemingly very willing to comply with the instruction, judging by his smile. 'With my help you will soon be first-class cook, *mademoiselle.*'

'I don't mean to stay long enough to get much practice,' Lisa informed him swiftly, and turned to face him. 'You can tell Mr ben Dacra that I don't intend to take a course in Cordon Bleu cooking because I'm not staying!'

Ali looked a little taken aback at her vehemence, and Lisa realised she was being rather unfair, taking it out on Ali when it was his employer who was at fault. 'Do you not wish me to help you, *mademoiselle?*' He could be as appealing as a puppy when he looked as he did now, and Lisa's heart relented. 'I am very good at cooking,' he insisted earnestly.

'Yes, I'm sure you are,' Lisa smiled.

'My *grandpère* was a French chef—very good; very famous!'

'Was he?' She looked suitably impressed, and Ali, satisfied that he was making headway, took up another knife and began helping to prepare the vegetables. 'I thought you were Moroccan, Ali, I didn't know you were partly French too.'

'You know about Monsieur ben Dacra?'

Lisa nodded, casting him a curious glance from the corner of her eye. 'Why? Is it supposed to be a secret?' She remembered that Geoffrey had found out only later about Yusuf's real father.

Ali shrugged. 'No, but not all people know. He looks as if he were Moroccan only, yes? And when he is wearing the *djellaba*——'

'I've seen him in the *djellaba*,' Lisa told him, and Ali's face split into a broad grin, as if something amused him hugely.

'Ah, *oui*,' he said. 'When Monsieur ben Dacra make you come aboard again at Bouli, eh?'

'I didn't find it particularly funny!'

He immediately sobered, but there was still a lurking mischief in his eyes, and Lisa guessed he would have enjoyed the sight of her being dragged ignominiously aboard the *Djenoun* by his employer. There seemed to be a streak of cruelty in Ali just as there was in Yusuf ben Dacra and she found it equally unacceptable in both of them.

They worked silently for a while, then she happened to catch his eye, and Ali smiled. That dazzling, crooked-toothed smile that was irresistible. 'You going to let me teach you to cook?' he asked, and Lisa pulled a face.

'I suppose so,' she agreed. 'Since your *grandpère* was a famous chef, it seems a pity to waste the opportunity.'

One eyelid fluttered briefly in a suggestion of a wink and he was smiling again. 'I have a little French, a little Spanish and a lot of Moroccan, *mademoiselle*, but like Monsieur ben Dacra, I choose to be Moroccan.'

'On the contrary, you're *noth*ing like Mr ben Dacra,' Lisa assured him, and left him in no doubt that she had paid him a compliment. 'I don't like domineering, ruthless tyrants like your Monsieur ben Dacra, and I mean to give him the slip the moment I get the chance!'

'You do not like him?'

The fact seemed to puzzle him, and Lisa wondered why. 'Is he so universally popular, then?' she countered. 'I can't imagine why!'

'Ladies like him,' Ali told her with a wicked roll of his eyes.

'And how about him?' Lisa asked, playing along for the moment. 'Does he like the ladies?'

'Oh, but yes!' Ali agreed, with more eye-rolling and a broad beaming smile. 'But Monsieur ben Dacra is discreet, you understand. Not as Monsieur Yacub Boudri, his brother—he has what you call a reputation, eh?'

Remembering the velvet dark eyes and slumbrous smile of the young man who had so obligingly got Yusuf to see her in the garden, Lisa nodded. 'Yes, I can imagine! But you mean adopted brother, don't you; they're not brothers, actually, are they?'

'Adopted brother; stepbrothers, all the same,' Ali guessed with a careless shrug. 'They all one family.'

Briefly, for she dared not appear too curious in case she put an end to his confidences, Lisa glanced at him from the corner of her eye. '*Are* they all one family? I couldn't sort it out.'

She gave the impression that she was much better informed than she was in fact, Lisa knew, but she excused herself by thinking it was unlikely to be a secret what actual relation Yusuf was to Sheik Abahn's sons. Unsuspectingly, Ali enlightened her.

'Madame married first the French engineer and then Sheik Abahn. Mademoiselle Zeineb is their daughter. So —all one family, yes?'

Lisa did see now, but she could understand why no one bothered to sort out the ben Dacra/el Boudri tangle of relationships. It was much simpler to class them all as one family. 'Do you like working for Mr ben Dacra?' she asked, wondering how honest he would be about that.

But there was no mistaking his sincerity when he answered her. 'Oh yes, *mademoiselle*. He is a very—good man, and everybody likes him. Also he pays good wages.'

'I don't doubt that.' Lisa accepted the fact of his paying his crew well, because she could imagine he would. That reputation for fair dealing that Geoffrey had mentioned would extend to his employees, she thought. But she wanted to know why else Yusuf ben Dacra was so well liked. 'But what makes you say he's good man, Ali? Why *good?* It isn't a term that's used very much these days, is it?' Ali looked puzzled, and shook his head as if he did not follow her reasoning. 'I mean take what he's doing at Zobi, for instance. How can you——'

'I know nothing about that, *mademoiselle*; excuse me!'

So he *had* been primed not to say too much to her, Lisa thought, and sliced through a bright red pepper with angry relish when she thought about it. Ali was ready enough to sing his praises, but adamantly refused to discuss the subject that interested her most.

'You're well trained,' she told him with a wry smile.

'But surely if it's common knowledge what's happening at Zobi, there's no harm in you talking to me about it.'

'I cannot do that, *mademoiselle*!'

'Because he's threatened——'

'Monsieur ben Dacra does not make threats, *mademoiselle*!' Ali's reproof had an unexpected dignity, and she could see he was quite adamant about not talking about Zobi, whatever reason he had.

'All right, I'm sorry.' She gave him a smile, though it was a rueful one. 'I won't embarrass you by asking any more questions about your master's plans for Zobi.'

'Thank you, *mademoiselle*—but Monsieur ben Dacra is my employer, not my master.'

Lisa wondered for a moment if he was completely serious about the correction; decided he was and apologised once more. 'No, of course he isn't; I'm sorry, Ali.'

From then on they got along splendidly. Lisa was ready to admit that Ali was not only a competent cook, but also a very able tutor, and she felt she had learned quite a lot by the time dinner was ready. Not only about cooking, but about Ali too. He was friendly and easy-going, but staunch in his loyalty to Yusuf ben Dacra, so that there was little hope of him doing anything to earn his disapproval; like helping her get away.

They were laughing together uninhibitedly about something Ali had said, when Lisa saw his expression change suddenly and swung round to see what had caused it. She should have known, she thought, when she saw Yusuf's towering form standing in the doorway, his black brows wearing an unmistakable frown of disappoval. He said something in Arabic; brief, but obviously to the point because Ali gave her a swift sideways glance and bobbed his head.

Dinner was almost ready so there was nothing more he could do, but Lisa resented the fact that he was being so summarily removed, as if by making her laugh he had committed some grave offence. 'Don't blame Ali,' she said, before Yusuf had time to say anything to her. 'He made me laugh, that's all. He hasn't been guilty of anything worse than cheering me up!'

At a brusque nod from his employer, Ali slipped past her and made for the door, but before he went he half-turned his head, and this time there was no mistaking the broad wink he gave her. Hastily avoiding his eye, Lisa hoped Yusuf had not seen it too, but in vain. When Ali passed him in the doorway Yusuf said something in Arabic, short and sharp, and Ali's good-looking young face looked crestfallen as he went hurrying off along the passage.

'Did you *have* to do that?' Lisa demanded, resentful on Ali's behalf and her own. 'You needn't worry that he'll say something he shouldn't! He closed up like a clam the minute I mentioned Zobi!'

'I would hope so,' Yusuf said quietly. 'I do not expect to have my business gossiped about by trusted employees.'

Feeling that she had somehow been firmly put in her place, Lisa twisted the knife she held round and round in her fingers. 'But it makes it all the more unreasonable that you sent him off with what I would guess was a telling-off,' she protested.

The dark eyes did not waver. 'You do not know Ali as I do. I reprimanded him for winking his eye at you as he did. A smile of encouragement is all that Ali needs to become very—friendly.'

Lisa's eyes scorned his explanation. 'And you sent him to teach me to cook! Thank you!'

From the doorway Yusuf watched her steadily for a moment before he replied, and while he stood there he ran the fingers of one hand over the back of his head. The same gesture he had used at lunch-time after he kissed her, and conveying the same suggestion of discomfiture.

'I expected to find you keeping him at arm's length,' he said, and when he caught her swift frown of puzzlement and disbelief. 'It was the impression I got from——'

It was unthinkable that he was actually uneasy, and yet the signs were unmistakable. Lisa's heart was thudding wildly for no good reason she could think of, except that she remembered the way he had kissed her and the devastating effect it had on her. Turning her back, she put down the knife and began cleaning the work-top.

'Well, now you know differently,' she said in a not quite steady voice. 'I just hope you won't say any more to Ali; he doesn't deserve it. And as it happens I didn't have to keep him at arm's length.'

She had not really intended that slight stress on 'him', but somehow it happened, and when Yusuf did not say anything, she turned back to look at him again. But he was gone and the door closed, although she had not heard a sound, and she could not imagine why she felt so disappointed about it.

Lisa had slept very little, although it had been after midnight when she went to bed. She had had so much on her mind that it was impossible to sleep, for right up until the last moment she had refused to believe that Yusuf ben Dacra would detain her overnight. Not until the rich throbbing of the engines became the only sound to disturb the silence on board had she been forced to believe it, and then she had felt apprehension for the first time, when she realised how completely isolated she was.

Through her window she had watched the moon make shimmering paths across the water, and fat stars glitter like diamonds scattered on dark velvet. A wonderful, romantic setting that brought only added bitterness when she considered her position. It had seemed such a long time since they left Casablanca, and such a long way back home.

Not long after Yusuf left her in the galley, Ali had come with a quite unexpected invitation to dinner, but she had sent him back with a polite but firm refusal and made do with the same lamb and rice the crew had. No doubt Yusuf had thought her both stubborn and foolish to deprive herself of the privilege, but Lisa had not felt like risking another incident like lunchtime.

It had been after midnight when someone knocked on her door, but by then she had become resigned to not being released before morning, and nothing else interested her but that. Not even Yusuf ben Dacra, she thought bitterly, was callous enough to turn her loose in the middle of the night to find her own way home, so without bothering to discover who it was she had walked over and very deliberately turned the key in the lock. Whoever it was and whatever he wanted could wait until morning.

Waking late, she lay for a while trying to realise where she was, and when she remembered, the fact seemed even more incredible. She felt like weeping with frustration and disappointment; she even thought of making a play for his sympathy by crying in front of him, but unless she had misjudged her stony-hearted captor, he was not going to be convinced by a sudden resort to tears.

There was a bathroom adjoining her cabin and she brushed an impatient hand across her eyes as she made her way across to it. A leisurely shower did a lot to bolster her morale, even though she had to get into the same clothes again, and she was zipping up her slacks when someone knocked on her door.

She paused in what she was doing and looked up

swiftly, staring at the door and frowning slightly. Maybe it was her caller of last night. But if it was Ali with an invitation to breakfast she was going to send him back with a firm refusal, just as she had last night, no matter how hungry she was. Yusuf ben Dacra was far too disturbing a table companion for her to readily repeat yesterday's experience.

But obviously in this instance she was not to be allowed to ignore the caller, for another knock followed swiftly on the first, jolting her into activity. Hastily fastening the zip, she called out as she went.

'All right, all right, Ali, I'm coming!' Flinging the door wide, she stared for a second in blank surprise at Yusuf ben Dacra. 'Oh,' she said, too taken aback to think of being tactful, 'I didn't expect you.'

His lean height and broad shoulders loomed impressively in the doorway and Lisa could not understand why her heart lurched so wildly at the sight of him. It was quite incredible the effect he had in the circumstances. He regarded her for a moment without speaking, but she should have known he would notice and recognise the shadows under her eyes as evidence of a restless night.

'Good morning, Miss Pelham. Did you sleep well?'

'I hardly slept at all,' Lisa told him, making no attempt to match his cool politeness. 'Although you can hardly be surprised at that when you consider how much I have to worry about.'

Light slacks and a white shirt made him appear darker and even less European than usual this morning. He was freshly shaven and his skin glowed, smelling of the after-shave she was beginning to associate solely with him. He was a dark and disturbingly sensual creature whom she found it increasingly hard to dislike, despite her determinedly unco-operative attitude.

Ignoring her present complaint, he ran his eyes over the rather crumpled slacks and shirt she wore, and the riot of thick uncombed hair that tumbled around her face. 'May I come inside?' he asked, and when she hesitated, eyeing him warily instead, he frowned. 'You complained yesterday of having nothing to change into,' he reminded her.

'I've only what I stand up in—thanks to you.'

'The situation is of your making,' Yusuf reminded her curtly, 'but it can be remedied. I had intended telling you last night, but you refused to have dinner with me, and it was very late when I thought about it again; you were already asleep.' He contemplated her boldly for a moment. 'Or else you had some other reason for not responding to my knock.'

'I'm not in the habit of answering knocks on my bedroom door in the middle of the night,' Lisa informed him shortly, knowing perfectly well that he would have heard her turn the key last night. 'Especially in the present circumstances.'

'You may quite safely do so this morning,' Yusuf suggested with a hint of impatience, and Lisa stepped back to let him come in, automatically following him across the cabin. 'May I?'

He indicated a pair of tall folding doors that Lisa had assumed led into another cabin. She had not bothered to discover how true it was once she had found the bathroom, and she watched curiously as Yusuf pointed to them. 'Yes, of course.'

'My sister used this cabin last,' he told her, 'and unless I know Zeineb less than I think I do, she will almost certainly have left something in her wardrobe that could be of use to you.'

'Your sister?'

The question was irresistible and there was no mistaking the meaning behind it. But Yusuf apparently decided to take it at face value, for he merely inclined his head to acknowledge the correction. 'My half-sister, since you prefer to be precise, *mademoiselle.*'

Feeling rather small, Lisa watched him open up the folding doors and reveal, not another cabin, but a deep clothes cupboard. There was a row of brass-handled drawers at one side and a long row of mostly empty hangers swinging from a wooden rail. Several of them, however, had dresses carelessly hung awry as if the owner could not be bothered taking care, and Yusuf eyed them critically.

They were quite simple cotton ones for the most part, although much too good to have been discarded by anyone except a woman who had no need to worry about replacing them. He opened the pedestal of drawers too, and Lisa saw various articles of lingerie, discarded with the same casual disregard.

'As I thought,' he remarked dryly. 'Zeineb always leaves some of her things behind, and in this instance her carelessness will serve a purpose.' Even while he was commenting on his sister's habits, he was taking explicit stock of Lisa's size and shape, with no hint of embarrassment and with the air of a connoisseur. 'You will probably find them a little too large for you,' he decided. 'Zeineb is taller and more—*dodue*. Our women are less inclined to slenderness than Europeans, but you should find something here that you can adapt.'

Lisa was eyeing him curiously, the question of replenishing her wardrobe forgotten for a moment. 'You speak as if you're *not* European,' she said; and quoted his own words at him. '*Our* women are less slender than Europeans, you said. Aren't you part French?'

His expression suggested that, just for a second or two, she had surprised him; then he shook his head slowly. 'It is evident that you know more about me than I realised, Miss Pelham, if you are aware of my French blood. It is not widely known that I am partly French.'

'Are you ashamed of it?'

He took the challenge with a slight narrowing of his eyes, but he kept his temper, or so it seemed to Lisa. 'No, *mademoiselle*, I am not ashamed of it. My mother married a Frenchman, but I scarcely knew my father, and I have always counted myself Moroccan, as she is. I was born here and it is my country, although I was educated entirely in France for my father's sake.'

She had not expected him to be so forthcoming, and Lisa found the subject an unexpectedly intriguing one, so that she followed it up unhesitatingly. 'I've noticed that you resort to French more often than you do to Arabic when your English fails you,' she pointed out.

It had not occurred to her what implication could be drawn from her obvious interest, until she looked up at him for a moment and saw something in his eyes that brought swift colour to her cheeks. 'You have evidently observed me very closely, *mademoiselle*.' His voice seemed deeper suddenly and was curiously affecting, touching something in Lisa's senses and bringing a sudden urgency to the pulse that beat at her temple. 'Is it perhaps a case of—know thine enemy?'

Quickly on the defensive, she sounded a little breathless. 'I'm interested in people in general,' she told him. 'Not you in particular, Mr ben Dacra.'

'Ah!'

Quite obviously he was not convinced and Lisa hastily returned to her own situation rather than become any deeper involved in discussing her reaction to him. 'I'm interested at the moment in when you're going to let me go home,' she said. 'Don't you think this has gone on long enough? You can't keep me much longer without there being an almighty rumpus, you know. I'll already have been missed, don't you realise that?'

'Yes, of course I realise it.' He made the admission so coolly that Lisa stared at him, for he seemed so unconcerned it was hard to believe. 'It has also occurred to me that while I have you, your friends are unlikely to put their threat into action at Zobi. Here, in my hands, you are a very useful form of insurance, *mademoiselle*.'

Lisa eyed him incredulously, seeing his intention clearly for the first time. He was very probably right about the group hesitating to go into action while she was still held aboard the *Djenoun*; but she could not imagine why he felt himself immune from high-level repercussions if he went on holding her. No matter how influential Sheik Abahn and his family were, they could not get away with detaining a foreign national for very long.

There must be some other reason than sheer arrogance to account for his staggering self-confidence, she felt, although she could not for the moment think what it might be. Uncertain what else to do, she resorted to vague threats. 'When my father gets to hear about this, then you'll see what will happen!' she warned. 'You said yourself he's quite an important man, and he won't let you get away with holding me hostage like this!'

He still did not turn a hair, but eyed her levelly, and did not even raise his voice when he spoke. 'Your father understands the position far more clearly than you do, *mademoiselle*, and he is satisfied that you will come to no harm while you are aboard the *Djenoun*.' Lisa stared at him open-mouthed, but he ignored her obvious disbelief and pressed on in the same cool, confident tone. 'I contacted him yesterday by radio-telephone,' he told her, 'and he has agreed that I act *in loco parentis* until such time as I can conveniently put you ashore.'

'But that's ridiculous!' Lisa's brain refused to function normally and she could only stare at him for a second or two, shaking her head slowly back and forth. 'I'm not a child, I'm a grown woman; no one has that sort of right over me, not even my father, whatever he told you. I'm twenty-two—nearly twenty-three, and responsible for my own actions! Whatever impression you've been given, I'm no longer under parental control!'

The dark eyes did not waver and a hint of a curl on the firm lips suggested he was unimpressed. 'In my country, Miss Pelham, a daughter is under the control of her father until she marries, and you have a saying, I believe—when in Rome, do as the Romans do, yes? You have behaved in this matter with a total lack of responsibility, which suggests you have had less parental control than you should; but if you consider that your years demand you be treated other than as a wayward child, then so be it. You will be treated as a young woman in need of a severe lesson in how to behave responsibly in a foreign country—*my* country. But whichever you are, child or woman, your father has asked my indulgence, and in the circumstances I have agreed.'

Her heart was thudding so hard that Lisa almost choked on its urgency. She had to believe that he had contacted her father as he said, for it was the kind of positive step he *would* take. But it was harder to accept that her father had been quite so co-operative as he suggested.

It made it harder when she realised that the situation was entirely of her own making, and she knew her father would have little sympathy with the aims of the group, any more than Yusuf ben Dacra did. He was also sufficiently knowledgeable about the country he lived in to trust a man of Yusuf's standing in almost any circumstances; though she was suspicious of his readiness to trust him with the care and safety of his daughter in this instance.

'Why should he trust you, a stranger, so readily?' she asked, and for a brief moment Yusuf's dark eyes seemed almost to pity her.

'Did you not know that my father and I have known John Pelham for many years?' he asked. 'He accepts my word that you will be safe, even though the situation is somewhat—unconventional.'

Lisa remembered that fierce, unexpected assault on her senses yesterday and assumed he had neglected to mention that to her father. If only she had paid more attention when her father spoke about his work, she might have gained an insight into the character of this dangerous adversary. As it was she was at a disadvantage. Yusuf had been able to lull him into a sense of security so that he had agreed to her being held incommunicado as an assurance of the group's good behaviour.

'What did you tell him?'

It did not matter now what he had told her father, but she needed time to think. She was again on the verge of crying in sheer frustration, but she saw no sign of relenting on Yusuf's dark face as he watched her.

'I told him how you had smuggled yourself aboard with some silly notion of warning me off the Zobi project, and that you were virtually a stowaway. I also told him that in exchange for my not informing the police and for keeping the whole matter as quiet as possible, you have agreed to remain on board and cook for my crew.'

'Blackmail!' Lisa accused bitterly and unhesitatingly, but Yusuf continued to eye her sternly and unwaveringly.

'It is nothing of the kind, Miss Pelham,' he denied firmly. 'Your father understands the delicacy of his own situation were this to become public knowledge. Zobi has government approval although it is our company's project. Any attempt to sabotage it will be seen as against our country's interests; and with foreign nationals involved the result could be very serious indeed; for those involved *and* their families.'

Suspecting that he was making it sound far more

serious than it was, Lisa nevertheless was bound to see some sense in his reasoning, though she admitted it reluctantly. And not at all to Yusuf ben Dacra. 'I rather think you're exaggerating,' she observed, far more casually than she felt. 'Daddy's too well known to your government for them to believe he's responsible for what I do.'

Dark eyes scorned her refusal to face facts, and clearly he had no intention of giving her the chance to change her mind. 'Whatever you feel, Miss Pelham, the fact remains that you are more useful to me as an insurance of your friends' good behaviour than you are free and getting into more mischief. In the circumstances your father feels I have been very lenient and he feels you will benefit from a little discipline. He is much happier knowing you are aboard the *Djenoun* rather than becoming further involved with your friends.'

'Oh, you've got it all nicely worked out, haven't you?' Lisa looked at him darkly, her eyes half-lidded and rebellious. 'I don't believe your government has an interest in building an hotel at the expense of a small community, and the group will go ahead, whether or not you hold me hostage. Don't you realise that?'

'I think not.' His gaze travelled slowly over her face and he shook his head, confident as ever. 'I understand there is a young man who will ensure their good behaviour; Geoffrey Mason? I would guess that he was the same young man who waited for you outside my father's house the other night. He cares enough about you to prevent the rest from acting irresponsibly, so I hear.'

'Oh, how *could* he!' Lisa despaired of what she saw as her father's treachery; of his readiness to side with authority as represented by one of Sheik Abahn's family. 'How could he entrust me to someone who sees me only as a hostage, and makes me wait on his crew as well!'

'You exaggerate,' he said coolly. 'Your father has

trusted me with the task of seeing that no harm comes to you, and I shall see that he has no cause to regret that trust.'

'Isn't it a little late for that?'

The reminder was unmistakable and Lisa saw the quick tightening of his lips, but his self-control was unwavering and she got little satisfaction from the jibe. He probably regretted that fierce, impulsive kiss far more than she did.

'This Geoffrey Mason is your lover?'

Lisa flushed and reacted more angrily because of it. He had no right to question her about Geoffrey or anyone else. 'No, he isn't!' she denied firmly. 'Geoffrey is a good friend, but that's all!'

'That is not your father's impression,' Yusuf observed, making it perfectly clear whose version he believed. 'However, now that you know your father has been informed and is satisfied, I am sure you will have less cause for anxiety.'

'It's no consolation to me! I want to go *home*!'

There was a certain pathos in the demand, but if Yusuf was affected by it he gave no sign. He consulted his watch, then indicated the open cupboards behind her. 'Take what you need,' he said. 'And then set about making breakfast for the crew. It is getting late and they too prefer to do their work with a full stomach.'

'Do I get Ali's help again?'

He shook his head firmly. 'No!'

He turned about and Lisa stared after him, glaring desperately at his broad unheeding back. 'How can you *do* this?' she demanded plaintively, and he turned just briefly in the doorway.

'Because you leave me no choice,' he said, and closed the door firmly behind him.

Lisa wore her borrowed clothes a little self-consciously,

for they were at least two sizes too big for her and it was difficult to disguise the fact. Really the dresses were much too good to be worn for kitchen work, but Lisa had little option but to make use of them, since she had no idea how long her enforced cruise was likely to last.

Her first choice had been a coral-red cotton with short sleeves and embroidered at the neck and hemline with white. She had chosen it partly because it was bright and cheerful and would be good for her morale, and partly because it brought out the golden tones in her skin and hair. She felt the need to look her best in her present circumstances.

When she first put it on it had hung like a sack on her slender form, but a scarf from Zeineb Boudri's discarded wardrobe served as a belt and pulled it in to fit, as well as making it a little shorter. The neck gaped and revealed rather too much cleavage, but there was little she could do about that, and Yusuf ben Dacra could hardly blame her in the circumstances.

Having supplied the crew's lunch she had eaten a little of the same meal herself. No invitation had been forthcoming, so seemingly Yusuf had taken her refusal last night as final. As on other occasions, as soon as the meal was cooked and served, she sought the cooler air on deck, leaning on the rail to watch the shoreline that seemed so tantalisingly near.

She actually thought it was nearer than ever today, but could not be sure, and there was no one she could ask. It was a different man at the wheel, but she was not optimistic enough to suppose he would be any more ready to defy his employer's instructions than his predecessor.

Nevertheless there was something about his wrinkled and weatherbeaten features that was not exactly discouraging, and she made her way along to the wheelhouse. The man acknowledged her rather tentative smile with one of his own, and Lisa took heart. '*Bonjour!*' she said.

She spoke no Arabic and very little French, but a lot of Moroccans spoke at least a little French, and perhaps her greeting would convey a feeling of friendliness. Evidently the elderly man was not one of them, for although he nodded in response, he made his reply in Arabic. Disappointed, but not entirely put off, Lisa stood in the narrow doorway of the wheelhouse and indicated what looked like a small town in the near distance, sprawling along the shoreline.

'What's that place called?' she asked, and narrowed her eyes against the harsh sun, trying to judge distances and shapes. 'Is it a town?'

She thought she could make out buildings, but not distinctly enough to be sure whether the place was a village or a town, or simply another port of convenience like Bouli, where she had so nearly escaped. The sun hurt her eyes if she stared too hard, and she looked to the man at the wheel to enlighten her, if he could.

Following the direction of her pointing finger he squinted his dark eyes into furrowed wrinkles of flesh and said something in Arabic, of which only one word meant anything to Lisa. When she heard it she turned her head again quickly and looked once more at the distant buildings shimmering in the heat. Heart thudding hard, she pointed again insistently while she repeated the name.

'Zobi? That's Zobi?'

The man nodded, looking at her curiously, and Lisa fidgeted with impatience because he did not speak English. It was just possible that an older man, probably a man with daughters, might have helped her if she could have made him understand her predicament. As it was, she sighed resignedly and moved back to the rail to stare into the distance, almost blinded by the glaring brassiness of the sun on water.

It was fascinating seeing the place that had come to mean so much to her in the past few days; the place she had risked so much for. It did not look very big at this distance, but Zobi was a village, not a town. There were only a very few palm trees, dotted like ragged mops along the skyline and suggesting that Zobi offered little in the way of shade; Lisa thought it looked a harsh and unfriendly site to build an hotel.

She was still gazing at it when she felt someone come up beside her, and she turned to find Ali at her elbow. '*Mademoiselle*.' He gave her a smile, but it lacked the beaming openness of the ones he had treated her to before, and it puzzled her. 'Monsieur ben Dacra wishes you to——'

'I'm not very interested in Mr ben Dacra's wants at the moment,' Lisa interrupted swiftly, unwilling to hear new instructions from her jailer. 'That's Zobi up ahead, isn't it, Ali?' He nodded, although it was clear he was not happy about having his employer's message ignored. 'The village of Zobi that we're making for?'

'That is so, *mademoiselle*.'

'We'll be putting in there—when? This afternoon? Tonight?' It was so difficult to tell just how far away they were, but Ali was almost sure to have some idea. 'When, Ali?'

He was cautious, and Lisa blamed Yusuf ben Dacra for putting him on his guard. 'This afternoon, I think, *mademoiselle*. But we shall not go into Zobi itself.' Lisa guessed he had volunteered the information because he had been unable to resist showing off his knowledge, and she looked at him encouragingly. 'It is not possible to take the *Djenoun* into Zobi because there is a sandbank that makes it impossible, you understand. So we must go a little more along the coast.'

Lisa looked along the deck to where the huge bulk of

the sacking-wrapped machinery they had taken on at Bouli loomed just aft of the wheelhouse, ugly and incongruous against the gleaming luxury of the *Djenoun*'s planking. 'What about that thing?' she asked, and Ali shrugged.

'The landing place is not more than one hundred metres from Zobi, *mademoiselle*. The machine can be driven across the sand quite easily.'

'Oh, I see.'

Lisa thought she was probably not being quite fair to question him as she was, but he was the only one of the crew who she knew spoke English. Also it had crossed her mind earlier that he might help her if she asked him, and she mused on the possibility again while he stood beside her, deciding to test his reaction.

'I'd give a lot to be able to go ashore when we get there,' she ventured. 'If I could just manage to——'

She left the sentence tantalisingly in the air, but Ali looked distinctly uneasy. His expression did not change, but his normally frank eyes were suddenly evasive, and Lisa wondered if he knew the predicament she was in, and why. Obviously if he did he was sufficiently in awe of his employer not to take any chances. He stood rather stiffly, carefully avoiding her eyes and returned to his original errand.

'I was to ask if you had eaten luncheon, *mademoiselle*,' he said. 'Monsieur ben Dacra is concerned that you eat properly.'

'I do.' Lisa dismissed the matter of her appetite and Yusuf's concern with the same slightly impatient gesture. 'But I'm far more interested in what's going to happen when we get to Zobi, Ali. Can't you tell me?' She had tried yesterday and failed, but she tried again.

'No, *mademoiselle*!'

Lisa first stared, then laughed shortly. Yusuf knew how to keep the loyalty of his crew, and she wondered just how he achieved it. 'Well, at least I know where I stand,' she said. 'It looks as if I'll have to rely on my own initiative yet again.'

'*Mademoiselle?*'

He looked puzzled, but Lisa wondered if he was quite so much in the dark as he made out. 'Never mind,' she said, and gave her attention again to the shimmering image of Zobi as it got closer with every minute. 'Well at least you could ask the helmsman exactly how long it will take us to get there, couldn't you?' she said.

Ali heaved his slim shoulders resignedly. He would not give anything away that Yusuf ben Dacra did not want her to know, she had discovered that already, but Ali was sympathetic to a point, she thought, and found comfort in that. He turned and was saying something to the man at the wheel, and once more the name Zobi was the only decipherable word in the spate of Arabic.

'About one half hour,' Ali told her, and Lisa frowned anxiously.

'So soon!'

She immediately thought of Geoffrey and the rest of the group already waiting at Zobi, and for some reason she did not understand, the hope persisted that they had changed their minds. She guessed that Geoffrey would be worrying about her, for she doubted if her father would have thought it necessary to put him completely in the picture. He had never liked Geoffrey very much and Lisa had never understood why, for he was exactly the kind of young man most parents would have approved of. Now that her father knew about Balek! he would feel his opinion justified.

'Has Mr ben Dacra said exactly what happens when we get to Zobi?' she asked Ali, but again he merely shrugged off the question.

'I cannot say, *mademoiselle*.'

'Or you won't!' Lisa retorted sharply, and Ali spread his hands regretfully.

'I am sorry, *mademoiselle.*'

Lisa sighed, turning from the sight of Zobi for a moment to look at him. Then she smiled ruefully and her eyes were more anxious than she realised. 'I suppose you can't even tell me if Zobi has a telephone or a post office, can you?' she asked, and Ali was shaking his head even before she had finished speaking.

'There is nothing, *mademoiselle*. It is a village of few people.'

'Of no people at all by the time your boss has finished vandalising it!' Lisa declared, and wondered that he could look so puzzled. He must surely have some idea of what was going on at Zobi. 'Is there any chance of me being able to find some form of transport out of there, apart from the *Djenoun?*' she asked, but with very little hope of him telling her.

Ali, it seemed, had co-operated as far as he intended to; he was shaking his head. 'I am sorry, *mademoiselle*, I cannot tell you.'

Shrugging impatiently, she turned to lean on the rail once more with her arms resting along the top of it, and when she heard the sound of Ali's retreating footsteps on the deck, she ignored it. He had more than likely gone back to report to his employer that she was showing a great deal of interest not only in Zobi itself, but in the possibility of finding transport out of there. Well let him. The thought of Yusuf knowing exactly what was behind her questions gave her a brief moment of satisfaction as she watched Zobi begin to take shape in the haze of heat. Let him have no doubt she would try again.

The nearer they got to Zobi the less impressive it looked, and Lisa frowned, undecided whether or not it was worth all the bother it had caused so far. Not to mention the worse trouble that could follow if Yusuf ben Dacra proved stubborn, and the group took the action they threatened to. It looked bare and inhospitable, and she could not imagine how anyone managed to survive there, or why they should want to stay.

She was still standing at the rail when the *Djenoun* turned quite sharply around the village itself and towards her mooring. It was isolated, as Ali had said, by a huge sandbank and the water swirled dangerously, stained brown by the sand sucked from the structure by the pull of a strong undertow—the kind of current that plagued this Atlantic coast for so much of its length.

Among the low shack-like buildings of Zobi she could see nothing to suggest that Geoffrey and the others had shown up, only a handful of workmen who took a moment from their labours to watch them in. It was no more than a hundred yards into a natural harbour that must once have been a small port, for it already possessed a jetty and was free of dangerous currents. So that Lisa wondered why Yusuf had not chosen that spot for his hotel instead of destroying Zobi.

Lisa was briefly distracted from the view on shore when she saw Yusuf striding across the deck, head down as if he meant business, but it took her only a moment to realise that he was not coming in her direction. At the moment he was concerned only with mooring his yacht, and she watched the procedure, quite fascinated by it.

His eyes seemed to be everywhere at once, checking distances and depths, nodding approval or issuing short, sharp orders, until the big shiny bulk of the *Djenoun* slid smoothly alongside the jetty, secured by her mooring lines and rocking gently on the swell. Only when the whole manoeuvre was completed did he seem to notice Lisa and come to where she stood at the rail, blowing smoke from his lips and flinging the end of his cigarette over the side as he came.

He said nothing for a moment, but stood looking down

at her with his disconcertingly steady gaze, as if he was trying to decide what to do with her. 'Obviously Zeineb's dresses *are* too big for you,' he said, and Lisa felt suddenly and inexplicably shy as she put a hand to the gaping neckline that showed far too much of her soft, lightly tanned skin.

The scarf that encircled her waist seemed suddenly to be pulled in much too tightly, and she was more conscious of the curves it emphasised, both above and below. And also of the fact that Yusuf's dark eyes lingered too long and too appreciatively on them, and brought a bright flush of colour to her cheeks.

It was a new experience for her to feel so completely overwhelmed by a man's admiration, and she was not yet sure whether she liked the sensation or not. 'There isn't much I can do about the neckline,' she explained in a huskily defensive voice, and gathered the offending opening into her hand for a moment. 'None of them has a high neck or I'd have worn it.'

'The colour suits you very well.'

The compliment, mild as it was, was so unexpected that Lisa did not quite know what to say. She was conscious of the thudding beat of her heart and of a curious shivery sensation that slid along her spine as he continued to watch her steadily.

'I suppose it matches my red-rebel image, doesn't it?' she suggested flippantly, and chanced a brief upward glance when she said it.

A lurking gleam in the depth of his eyes stirred strange and disturbing emotions in her, and she felt more self-conscious than ever in the badly-fitting dress. 'I find it curious,' Yusuf said in his deep and oddly affecting voice, 'that just by wearing a dress that is a few sizes too large for you, you appear so small and vulnerable.'

Lisa stroked her unsteady hands over the red dress and gave him a tentative smile. It was too much to hope that he might be relenting, and yet he had never before spoken to her as he did now and she could not help feeling hopeful. 'I *am* vulnerable at the moment,' she told him, and watched his face anxiously for a reaction. 'I'm very unsure what you intend to do with me, or how long you propose keeping me.'

Yusuf continued with his study of her for a few more seconds, then put a hand on her arm. His palm was hard and warm and it tingled on her soft skin so that she felt herself trembling again and wanting more than anything for him to go on being as nice to her as he was now.

'For now I would like you to go below to your cabin,' he told her, and surprise and disappointment made her draw back her arm sharply.

She could not understand the feeling she had of wanting to cry, because really nothing had changed. But for those few moments it had all been different; he had treated her like a woman instead of a very unwelcome disruption in his routine, and she had liked it. She could do no other than admit it, but it made his return to normal all the harder to take. And it made her angry; both with herself for being so responsive, and with him for making her so vulnerable.

'I'm not a prisoner,' she insisted in a voice that wavered uncontrollably. 'You can't lock me up, my father never intended you to do that!'

She struggled when he took her arm more firmly and guided her towards the companionway, but she knew it was useless. 'I do not intend to lock you up,' he assured her, urging her down the steps in front of him. 'As you say, you are not a prisoner, but you are under restraint as a stowaway and a would-be saboteur. If you give me your word, however, that you will make no more silly attempts to leave the *Djenoun*, I will not find it necessary to put someone on guard to make sure you do not leave.'

'Couldn't I have stayed on deck?' she asked. 'You could have kept just as strict an eye on me there.'

Yusuf was shaking his head. 'There is a great deal of activity on deck and no room for spectators.' She was ushered along the passage and into her cabin by the relentless hand under her arm. 'Please remain here until we have unloaded.'

'And what then?' Lisa demanded, turning to face him.

Standing in the doorway, Yusuf eyed her for a moment. 'And then, Miss Pelham, I hope you will relent sufficiently to have dinner with me.'

Lisa was still too startled to reply when he closed the door, and she dropped down on to the edge of the bed, blinking across at the closed door almost as if she expected him to reappear. But she could hear his footsteps retreating along the passage, and she could not imagine why she felt so excited at the prospect of having dinner with him. She was, after all, still his prisoner, even though he hadn't locked her in.

CHAPTER SIX

HER second night aboard the *Djenoun* Lisa slept soundly. It was due in part, she supposed, to the fact that she no longer felt quite so completely cut off, now that her father knew where she was. Although she was very disappointed that he had co-operated so readily with Yusuf ben Dacra.

She had also had several glasses of a fairly potent wine with her dinner which had helped to lull her into a less belligerent mood. In fact dinner with Yusuf had gone very smoothly and once or twice she had found herself wishing the circumstances were different, for she had quite enjoyed herself.

Not that last night's more congenial atmosphere meant that she was prepared to accept things as they were from now on; far from it. This morning she was as determined as ever to get ashore if it was at all possible, whether or not a truce had been called last night, and no matter what her father had agreed to. She owed it to Geoffrey, for he would be worrying about her.

With nothing to do until it was time to prepare lunch, Lisa took up her favourite stand on deck, but kept in the shade because the sun was much too hot to stand in it for any length of time. Another delve into Zeineb Boudri's wardrobe had produced a brightly patterned garment that was most likely meant to be worn with trousers.

On its original owner it was probably a three-quarter-length tunic, but on Lisa it came to just above her knees and served perfectly well for a dress, even if it was rather skimpy and showed more of her bare tanned legs than an ordinary dress would have done. It was loose and flowing and it had wide sleeves and a vee neck, and Lisa found it beautifully cool and comfortable, so that she did not bother to tie anything around the waist.

Brushing a stray wisp of hair from her forehead, she stood on tiptoe for a moment to look across at the shore, the other side of the jetty where the *Djenoun* was moored. The movement made the too-wide neck of the tunic slip down off one shoulder and she did not bother to recover it, but simply relished the hot dry air on her skin.

It was just possible to see Zobi from the deck of the *Djenoun* and she searched in vain for some indication that the group had put in an appearance. All she could see was Yusuf's workmen, clad in loose, striped, homespun *djellabas*, and unhurriedly piling bags of cement and stacking bricks. There was no sign of anyone else, and she frowned as she narrowed her eyes against the sun.

She could only assume that Geoffrey and the rest were holding off as Yusuf had suggested they might, until they were sure exactly what her position was on board the *Djenoun*. It was perfectly possible that Geoffrey was keeping the group in check until they were a little better informed and she fretted at her inability to contact them. How long they would hold off, she would not care to guess, for they had the Zobi project very much at heart, and she wondered just how long Yusuf ben Dacra could get away with the present situation; even with her father's co-operation.

'Tomorrow we shall start work on the demolition.' The words were said, very quietly, quite close to her ear, and Lisa turned swiftly, catching her breath. Recognising the advantage of surprise, Yusuf's eyes gleamed darkly. 'I startled you?'

Without admitting it, Lisa passed the tip of her

tongue swiftly across her lips before she answered him. Even in the full light of day there was something incredibly affecting about him, and he looked so very much at home against this hot, fierce background that just for a moment she felt herself shiver.

'You don't intend to heed our warning, then?'

Leaning on the rail beside her, Yusuf shook his head and reached out a hand to slide the neckline of the dress up on to her shoulder again. 'Have I not said so?' His eyes narrowed against the glare, he looked across at the site, while Lisa coped with the sudden increased urgency of her pulse. 'You are my insurance, Miss Pelham, and apparently an effective one, for I see no sign of your friends so far.'

'Oh, they'll be here,' Lisa declared hastily. 'They're probably keeping a low profile for the moment until they know how the land lies, but they'll be here. And make no mistake about it, I shall try every way I can to get away from you, whatever my father says!' The glint of mockery in his eyes for a moment angered her, and her own eyes flashed at him indignantly. 'You may find it amusing now,' she warned him, 'but you won't stop us, you know! We *are* in earnest, no matter how much you laugh at us!'

'I do not find it amusing, *mademoiselle*, I can assure you,' he informed her shortly. 'This whole ridiculous situation need never have arisen but for you and your silly, misguided group of friends interfering in something you know nothing about! I am not amused, Miss Pelham, I am angry because you have wasted my time and tried my patience to the point of exhaustion!'

'Then you should believe we mean what we say! We *are* in earnest, as I said.'

She looked, and felt, very small as she stood there defying him, and she was very much aware of how skimpy the bright coloured tunic was, and how much slim bare leg it showed. Yusuf's dark, angry gaze seemed to see so much more than she wanted him to, and his mouth had a faintly derisive smile that she did not like the look of at all. He was an alarmingly sensual man, and the more she was in his company the more apparent it became.

'You are a very lovely young woman,' he observed with stunning matter-of-factness, and his voice touched a responsive chord in Lisa's senses. 'But beautiful women should content themselves with being beautiful and not become too intense about earnest causes to the exclusion of everything else. If they do, *ma chère mademoiselle*, they can become very tiresome—you are, unfortunately, rapidly approaching that stage.'

Lisa flushed but clung to the remnants of her self-control because he seemed set on making her lose her temper. 'If you find me so tiresome, why don't you put me ashore?' she demanded.

He could prick her vanity more easily than any man had done before and she resented it fiercely. A compliment was no compliment if it was immediately followed by such a scathing remark, and she watched him in helpless anger while he reached into his pocket for a cigarette, and lit it.

'I see no purpose in going through that again,' he told her, and raised his head from the lighter-flame to look at her narrow-eyed. 'May I suggest that you return to your kitchen duties, Miss Pelham? I have received no complaints from my crew about your cooking, so presumably you have at least one feminine attribute—you are a passable cook.'

'Thank you!'

She responded with heavy sarcasm, but in fact it was startling to realise just how much his scathing comments hurt, and she was trembling with a tangle of emotions he had aroused in her, and which she did not pretend to understand. She felt angry and confused and she regretted that last night's brief truce had once more degenerated into open warfare, but she had little hope of getting the better of him if she tried to hit back. He was too confident of his own rightness.

'If I was as amenable and—and submissive as you think I should be,' she told him bitterly, 'I'd have no chance at all against a—a tyrant like you.' She was appalled to realise just how close she was to tears; tears not only of anger but of regret too, but she could not yield now. Her voice was husky and unsteady, but she stood her ground rather than blindly obey his injunction that she should go back to the galley. 'The least you could do is let me go ashore for an hour.'

Yusuf looked beyond her to the hot dusty site of his project and he shook his head. 'I think not, Miss Pelham. Not until I am certain that your friends no longer present a threat to my plans.'

'But that's not feasible!' Her eyes brimmed with the tears that she was determined he should not see, and she held herself tightly under control. 'It can take months, even years, to complete a project like that!'

He held her wavering gaze steadily, his lips pursed to emit a thin jet of smoke. 'I doubt if your friends' enthusiasm will last so long,' he said. 'But I shall keep you here for as long as is necessary.' There was an air of ruthless determination about him that Lisa noted with a hammering heart. 'Perhaps by then,' he went on, 'you will have learned to care for other things than interfering in matters about which you know nothing.'

'I care about Zobi and what you're proposing to do to it!' Lisa insisted, but her voice shivered uncertainly and Yusuf was still watching her as he drew on his cigarette.

'You care about putting on a show,' Yusuf insisted relentlessly. 'You know nothing about Zobi or its people;

if you did you would not have set out on this ridiculous escapade.' His arrogant head at an angle, he looked down at her with gleaming dark eyes. 'And now I shall insist that you return to your duties in the galley. It is getting late and my crew are accustomed to having their meals on time. I have a certain reputation for being a good man to work for, and I do not intend to lose that reputation on your account.'

'If you think——' Lisa began. But he had already turned away, leaving her to glare in angry frustration at his retreating back. In the circumstances there was little else she could do but as he said.

It was nearly two days later when Yusuf found her on deck once more; leaning on the rail and looking as disconsolate as she felt. She had refused to join him for another meal and Yusuf had not pressed the matter, although Lisa thought Ali was rather disappointed. Whether or not Yusuf really minded, she had no idea, and there was little likelihood of her finding out.

Her pulse fluttered rapidly when he came up beside her, but she did not turn her head, nor did she break the silence between them, but left it to him. Although what he said was hardly what she expected and took her by surprise. 'Do you know Tiznit?' he asked.

Lisa turned her head quickly, and her eyes were at once eager and anxious, for the question was not merely an idle one, she felt sure, and something in his voice raised her hopes. 'I know *of* it,' she said, and a slight huskiness in her voice betrayed the anxiety she was trying so hard not to show. 'Why?'

His narrowed gaze went beyond the sandy foreshore of Zobi and to the hazy distance. 'It is only a few kilometres from here,' he said, and Lisa's heart began a quick tap-tapping against her ribs as she watched his face, trying to read what was going on behind his eyes when he switched his gaze back to her. 'It occurred to me that you might perhaps enjoy a drive as far as Tiznit.'

'Oh yes, I would!' She made no pretence of being other than in favour of the idea and her blue eyes sparkled between their thick brown lashes. 'Now?'

'Very soon, anyway.'

She glanced down at the brightly coloured tunic that showed off her slim bare legs. 'Only I'm not really fit to be seen in this dress.'

Yusuf took stock of it with his usual frank appreciation, and seemed to find nothing wrong with what he saw. 'You are perfectly fit to be seen in that dress,' he argued in his quietest voice, and one hand slid the wandering neckline back up on to her shoulder as he had done before, and with the same disturbing effect. The lingering touch of his fingers on her flesh brought a brief, shivering reaction from her that was impossible to control. 'But perhaps in the circumstances it would be better to change into your own clothes,' he suggested. 'You have plenty of time.'

'Who'll be taking me?' Lisa wanted to know in a distinctly unsteady voice. 'You?'

She had a curious little curling sensation in her stomach when she anticipated driving with him and, had she thought about it, it would have surprised her to realise that the idea of it as a means of escape did not even occur to her. She thought only of going ashore and going to see a place she had heard of but never visited, and she watched a brief smile touch his mouth as he bent his head to light a cigarette.

'Does that make you want to change your mind about going?' he challenged softly, and Lisa shook her head.

'No.' She sounded very sure of it. 'I'd like to go to Tiznit whoever takes me.'

There was amusement in his eyes for a moment, but not mockery in this instance, she felt sure. 'You are thinking about the glamour of the desert oasis, is that it?' he asked. 'Tiznit is on the very edge of the Sahara—it *is* an oasis, although perhaps not just as you picture it.'

Still slightly on the defensive, Liza kept her eyes on Zobi rather than meet that steady and infinitely disturbing gaze. 'The desert fascinates most people who haven't seen it,' she insisted. 'I suppose because we've nothing like it in Europe.'

'It also fascinates those who know it well,' Yusuf told her.

Lisa wondered just how familiar *he* was with the lonely fascination of the Sahara. His hawkish profile and teak-brown skin suggested he had much more in common with his Moroccan mother's family than with his European father, and when she turned her head and looked up at him briefly, a shiver of sensation slid along her spine.

'Are you one of those who know it well?' she asked.

'Quite well.' He expelled smoke from pursed lips and his eyes were for the moment half-hidden by black lashes, but he seemed willing enough to enlighten her. 'My mother's people were originally of the R'Guibat tribe and some of them still keep to the old nomadic life. I have visited them, when my grandparents were alive and they came into Goulimine.'

'The R'Guibat?' Lisa looked at him curiously, recalling where she had heard the name before, and Yusuf nodded.

'The Blue Men,' he said. 'You know of them, of course.'

'Yes, of course.' It occurred to Lisa suddenly how very different he seemed when he was talking about something other than business or her own shortcomings. 'It's a pity we're not going as far as Goulimine.'

He drew deeply on his cigarette for a moment, then threw the rest of it over the side into the sea before he spoke. 'When I have attended to the business I have in

Tiznit we can drive on to Goulimine for an hour if you would like to,' he said, and Lisa could not imagine why her heart was suddenly beating so hard and fast that she felt as if she had run a very long way. 'Would you like to do that?'

'Yes; yes, of course I would, I'd love it.' She was rubbing a forefinger back and forth on the top of the rail and thinking of what he said, a small thoughtful frown between her brows. 'Did you say you have business in Tiznit?'

He nodded. 'I have, but it will not take very long to complete.'

The prospect of the drive and the visits to Tiznit and Goulimine were suddenly put into perspective, and Lisa began to wonder about the real motive for his asking her to go with him. He could have left her aboard the *Djenoun* while he attended to his business, but there was always the chance that she would outwit his crew and manage to go ashore. If he kept her under his own more diligent eye he could be sure of her not getting away—it was logical, and above all Yusuf ben Dacra was logical. But while she watched her finger move across the rail she found herself almost praying that it was not his only reason for asking her.

'What would have happened if I'd said I didn't want to go with you?' she asked in a slightly breathless voice, her finger rubbing harder and harder.

Reaching over, Yusuf placed his own big hand over hers; his long brown fingers pressing gently for a moment. 'Then I should have been very disappointed,' he said, and Lisa closed her eyes briefly in undeniable relief.

For the first time since she had known him, she smiled up at him openly and frankly. 'In that case,' she said, 'I'd better go and change.'

Yusuf had been right; Tiznit was not what she expected

it to be, but Lisa was not disappointed by any means. From a distance it did not look quite real, but more like a stage setting than an actual town. A gated town with ramparts and towers and the fan-like spread of palm trees against the skyline, it delighted Lisa long before she saw it close to.

She had a little while on her own to explore, but not very long, for, as he had promised, Yusuf's business, whatever it was, took up very little time. Having completed it he came in search of her and found her, by some unerring instinct, admiring one of the six gates that gave access to the fortifications.

He had evidently done some shopping too, for he carried a couple of smallish packages tucked under one arm. Lisa made no objection when he suggested they leave, for he had already told her it was some distance to drive to Goulimine. But sitting beside him in the Land-Rover once more she eyed him curiously as he started up the engine.

'You don't *mind* going on to Goulimine, do you?' she asked, and he half-smiled, turning those dark, unfathomable eyes on her for a moment.

'I should not have volunteered to take you there if I had not wished to go,' he promised her frankly, and Lisa thought she was beginning to know him well enough to be sure he meant what he said.

It was, as he said, quite a long drive; much longer than Lisa had realised, but they had started fairly early in the day and not stayed over-long in Tiznit, so they could still be back on the *Djenoun* by nightfall, all being well. As yet the irony of that speculation did not strike her, and she settled back to enjoy the drive.

The route took them to the Tizi Mighert Pass and through a veritable forest of thorny argan trees where goats ignored the thorns to go scavenging among the branches for juicy leaves. But then they left the trees behind and there was no more vegetation at all; when even the last treeless hillocks of the Anti-Atlas petered out and gave way to a seemingly endless plain, Lisa felt the first impact of the barren desert.

It was her first experience of such over-aweing vastness and she found it rather unnerving, so that when the lushness of a palm grove appeared in the distance ahead of them, she heaved an inward sigh of thankfulness. 'An oasis?' she ventured, and Yusuf once more half-turned to look at her.

'Not yet Goulimine,' he said. 'That lies just beyond those palm groves; about fifteen kilometres beyond.'

'That far?'

He smiled at her obvious surprise. 'It will not seem so long, you will find,' he promised, and eyed her quizzically. 'How do you feel about your first glimpse of the desert?'

Lisa hesitated to commit herself too soon. 'I find it—over-aweing,' she confessed, and saw the way he smiled.

'But this is not the place to judge it,' he told her. 'Here it is only a promise of what the desert is like. The real Sahara lies beyond Goulimine.'

'Where your mother's people still live,' she remembered, and Yusuf nodded, but said nothing.

It was not long afterwards that they drove into Goulimine itself; inside the impressive walls that completely enclosed the town, and in to a place of sandy-red houses built of dried desert mud. It was a little bigger than Lisa had imagined it, and more commercial too, although not in the same way as the more Westernised towns and cities of the north.

There were a couple of hotels and restaurants catering for European tastes, but primarily it was still a desert town, a harbour in the sea of sand. It was the market town of the R'Guibat tribe who each Saturday and Sunday drifted into Goulimine for their weekly *souk*, and became the centre of interest for a growing tourist industry.

Lisa had heard about the Blue Men—the tribe who for the past four hundred years, ever since an English merchant introduced them to an indigo-dyed cloth, had dressed in the same distinctive blue robes and turbans from which the dye spread to colour even their skins blue, a phenomenon that made them easily distinguishable from any other of the desert people. She was only sorry that this was not a week-end and they would be unable to witness the arrival of the intriguing nomads from whom Yusuf's mother had come.

But if she could not see the Blue Men, there were plenty of other things for her to see, including plenty of shopping arcades. Shops selling all the traditional craft-made items that were the very life-blood of Morocco. Coppersmiths and leather workers lived in the intriguing red mud houses, alongside the makers of the gold and silver jewellery, and all sold their products in the arcades of Goulimine.

It all fascinated Lisa, but she saw one item that particularly took her eye and she lingered over it for so long that it was obvious it attracted her more than anything else. It was a heavy silver bracelet, like the desert women wore; primitive in design but still breathtakingly beautiful, and Lisa found it hard to walk away.

'You like that?'

She glanced up to find Yusuf's face hovering close to her own and he indicated the bracelet she was admiring with an inclination of his head. Lisa nodded, not for a moment suspecting what result her admission would have. 'I couldn't say why exactly,' she confessed with a shivering little laugh that admitted a weakness. 'I adore this kind of thing. It's very primitive, even crude, but it's also beautiful.'

From the way he smiled, Lisa guessed that her opinion

pleased him, but only when he called for the attention of the shopkeeper did it begin to dawn on her what he had in mind, and she caught her breath. Shaking her head, she tried to interrupt, but in vain. For one thing it was not easy to interrupt Yusuf ben Dacra, and for another he was already bargaining with the man, as custom demanded.

Using hands and arms in a flurry of extravagant gestures, the two men haggled amiably, words flying backwards and forwards over the bracelet that lay gleaming richly and temptingly on Yusuf's broad palm. Again Lisa tried to intervene before it was too late, but Yusuf waved her smilingly to silence, and the bargaining continued.

Eventually a price was reached that satisfied both parties, and Yusuf took out his wallet, handing over the required number of *dirhams* while Lisa stood by anxiously. She knew she hadn't enough money to pay for it herself, and she was very doubtful about allowing him to buy it in the circumstances.

'You can't do this,' she murmured breathlessly. The sharp dark eyes of the jeweller were on them, curious and intrigued by the contrasts between his two customers; the man so tall and dark and the girl so small and fair, and Lisa was conscious of it. 'It isn't——'

'You would prefer another one?' Yusuf countered swiftly, but his eyes made it clear that he knew that was not her reason for objecting.

'I mean I didn't intend buying one at all.'

His back half-turned to the seller, Yusuf reached for her hand and slid the silver bracelet over her hand and on to the slender wrist, his fingers caressingly light on her skin. 'You have *not* bought it, hah?'

Still in a daze and not knowing quite what to say, Lisa stared at it, twisting the heavy, cool silver round and round on her wrist while Yusuf watched her with a curiously gentle look in his eyes. 'You can't—I mean, I can't let you buy anything like this,' she insisted, and tried hard to stifle the thrill of pleasure it gave her to wear the gift. 'It's very beautiful and I love it, but I've never taken presents from men——' She had so nearly said men-friends, and she suspected he knew why she had stopped short so suddenly. 'I suppose that sounds illogical to you, doesn't it?'

There was a hint of defensiveness in her voice and his expression suggested he regretted it. 'I hope you will make an exception in this case,' he said, too quietly for the proprietor of the jewellery shop to hear. 'It would be a pity to deprive yourself of something you want so much, simply for an old-fashioned principle.'

Lisa looked up at him, her lips parted, ready to remind him that he had been the one in favour of old-fashioned principles, surely. But he met her eyes and something in the depths of his kept her silent. Instead she examined the bracelet, turning it round and round. It was curious how suggestive it was of a shackle when she looked at it more closely, and it was heavy too, but she knew that not for anything would she have parted with it now.

'It's beautiful,' she said. 'Thank you.'

She had the idea he was smiling, although she did not look up again. Walking with him through the cool shadowed arcades gave her a sense of rightness suddenly, and it was a sensation she made no attempt to find a reason for.

By the time they got back to the *Djenoun* it was already dark, and the view as the Land-Rover bumped along the last few metres of the sandy track to the mooring struck Lisa as almost too perfect. Nothing particularly spectacular had happened to make her feel as she did, but she felt that somehow everything had changed in the few hours she had been away. Not once had they exchanged angry words, and Yusuf had been a willing and knowledgeable guide, but apart from his buying her the silver bracelet which still encircled her wrist, nothing had happened to account for her feeling so oddly satisfied.

The moon was a little past full and it shone in rippling streaks across the surface of the sea, golden as honey and in smooth contrast to its reflection. It looked so idyllically romantic seen through Zobi's fringe of ragged palm trees that she could forget for a moment the squat little houses whose fate she had so determinedly argued about with Yusuf.

Her sigh was barely audible, but Yusuf must have heard it, for he turned his head briefly and looked at her before braking to a halt and getting out. 'You regret coming back?' he asked as he slipped a helping hand under her arm.

Lisa stepped out on to the stone pier and stood for a moment while he turned off the vehicle lights and took a couple of packages he had brought from Tiznit from the back seat. 'I suppose I do,' she admitted, walking beside him along the pier. 'After all, I am still your prisoner, even though I've been able to forget it for an hour or two today.'

Hooking a finger through the bracelet on her wrist, he lifted her captive arm up between them. 'Did I not threaten to put you in irons?' he asked, and it was Lisa who laughed so uninhibitedly as they approached the *Djenoun.*

The gangway was down, but there was no one about, only the lights burning comfortingly against a background of moonlit sea, and Lisa wondered that there was no one on deck. They neither saw nor heard anyone until Ali emerged from the shadows by the companionway suddenly.

He bobbed Lisa a brief bow, then addressed himself

in Arabic to his employer. But if his aim was to keep Lisa from knowing what he was saying, he was not altogether successful, for somewhere in the spate of Arabic she caught the unmistakable sound of Geoffrey's name, recognisable even in Ali's strong accent.

She looked at Yusuf anxiously, wondering why she suddenly felt so anxious to know that Geoffrey and the rest of the group had not put in an appearance while they had been away. Tentatively she placed a hand on Yusuf's arm and he turned quickly, frowning slightly as if he wondered how far he could trust her. After the past few hours of amiable truce it was hard to be back to normal and she regretted it more than she cared to admit.

'Is Geoffrey here?' she asked, and her lack of enthusiasm must have struck Yusuf as odd. 'I thought I heard Ali say——'

'He *was* here,' Yusuf told her shortly. 'He arrived shortly after we left, but he was alone and asking to see you—demanding to see you.' He sounded as if he had a perfect right to object to anyone demanding to see her, and Lisa was too unsure of her reaction to say anything. 'It is as I thought,' Yusuf went on confidently. 'Your being here is a deterrent.'

'The others didn't come to Zobi at all?' She felt horribly treacherous for speaking as she did; as if she was anxious for the rest not to follow Geoffrey.

'No one saw them,' Yusuf told her. 'I think it is safe to assume that your—friend was here alone because he is more personally involved than the rest. Or perhaps he was on a reconnaissance; trying to discover how safe it is for them to proceed. With luck he will have been discouraged enough to suggest calling the whole thing off.'

But Lisa was less convinced and she looked across at the site, her brows drawn anxiously. 'I doubt it very much; they have the fate of Zobi very much at heart, and I don't think the fact that you're holding me hostage will keep them off for good.'

Beyond the stone pier Zobi appeared closer at night than by day, when the heat made a distorting haze even at that short distance. A couple of lamps hung from two of the palm trees and a fire had been lit in the open at the edge of the village. It looked quiet and incredibly peaceful, with an occasional shadowy figure passing across the firelight, and Lisa regretted that it was the cause of such controversy.

She had not anticipated feeling as she did when it came to the point, and she could not quite understand why she found herself anxious that nothing should disturb the peace of Zobi and bring a heartfelt but so far purely verbal objection to the point of violent action. She realised that she had come into the situation with preconceived ideas, and not all of them were as clearly cut as she had thought. She felt very small and uncertain, and inextricably involved in a situation that threatened to get out of hand very soon now, and it was somehow instinctive to turn to Yusuf.

'I—I don't like the idea of a pitched battle,' she ventured, and he looked down at her steadily for a moment before he replied.

'I doubt very much if it will come to that,' he told her. 'Your friends will have sense enough to know that they cannot win, when they realise that they have both the site crew and the crew of the *Djenoun* to deal with if they come.'

Lisa glanced around her uneasily, realising at last the reason for the *Djenoun*'s feeling of desertion, and she shrank from the idea of him mustering his men for a full-scale conflict in defence of his property. Looking up at his face with its shadowed dark eyes, she nervously moistened her lips.

'You've sent them all over to Zobi in case the group

come in force?' she asked, and Yusuf's gaze challenged her darkly.

'*Will* they come in force?' he countered softly and, trying to read what was going on behind those unfathomable dark eyes, Lisa hesitated.

'I don't know.' A mere glimpse of movement at the corner of his mouth brought her head up swiftly and she spoke quickly and urgently, anxious to convince him. 'I *don't*, I honestly don't! Please believe me.'

'Would you tell me if you did? Yusuf demanded in the same softly persuasive voice, and she shook her head; a short jerky movement that showed how reluctant she was to answer.

'I don't know that either,' she confessed.

For what seemed like an interminable time he watched her small, anxious face, then he shook his head. 'I do not think they will do anything tonight at least,' he told her, and when she glanced up quickly to remind him that he had sent his men over there in force, she noticed he was smiling, and his eyes gleamed darkly at her between their black lashes. 'With my men over there to ensure nothing happens, we may enjoy our dinner on deck in the moonlight without fear of interruption.' His voice dipped a full octave as he bent his head slightly. 'Unless you refuse to dine with me, Lisa.'

Lisa made no pretence of even thinking about refusing, for her heart was beating hard and fast and her legs felt oddly unsteady, so that she needed something to cling to as she tried to sound cool and unaffected. Looking down at the trousers and shirt she had worn all day, she wished she had something more glamorous to wear for a moonlight dinner on deck with him; but his sister's wardrobe did not run to evening dresses.

'I won't refuse,' she told him, in a not quite steady voice. 'It sounds like a pleasant way to end a very pleasant day.'

His eyes had a deep gleaming darkness in the moonlight, and she told herself she was much too susceptible. Indicating that she should precede him down the companionway, Yusuf followed her, his feet taking the steep steps with much more confidence than her own more careful ones. 'What will you wear?' he asked, and she turned and looked over her shoulder at him as he followed her along the passage to her cabin. Coming to a halt outside her cabin door she turned to face him, but he was pushing one of the packages he carried into her hands before she could answer. 'You have been wearing Zeineb's clothes,' he said. 'I see no reason why you should not continue to do so.'

'What is it?'

He smiled at her suspicion. 'Take it,' he urged. 'I always buy Zeineb something whenever I go away, and I got her a *caftan* while I was in Tiznit. It does not matter that such a garment is a little too big.'

'Oh, but I can't take a present that you bought for your sister,' Lisa protested. 'Not even to borrow it.'

'Of course you will wear it,' Yusuf insisted. 'Zeineb has no need of a new *caftan*, and you have need of something to help your morale—she would be the first to insist that you wear it.' Looking down at her in the dim lighting of the passage, his eyes glowed darkly. 'To please me?' he murmured persuasively, and Lisa held the soft package tightly while she sought for the door handle with her free hand. 'I just hope you're right.' Her hands were trembling and she felt oddly lightheaded when she recalled that he had made her take the gift for her comfort and pleasure, and she whispered hasty thanks as she turned the handle and opened the door. 'Thank you, Yusuf.'

Her use of his name had been quite automatic and she did not even realise she had used it until he took her hand from the door handle and raised it to his mouth.

'De rien, ma chère,' he said softly, and pressed his lips to her fingers.

Lisa did not remember when she had felt so good in anything as she did in the *caftan* that Yusuf had insisted she wear. It was made of a deep rich red brocade embroidered in silver and black, and it made her light skin appear almost translucent by contrast. Considering it had been bought for someone who was two sizes bigger than she was, it fitted her well, although the flowing lines of it suggested rather than emphasised the shape beneath it.

The only mirror in the cabin was inside the door of the wardrobe and she pushed it wide to enable her to admire her new image speculatively, before she went to join Yusuf on deck. It was just the right length and it was when she saw her toes peeping from below it that she frowned suddenly. Running her hands down over the richness of the material, she eyed her reflection thoughtfully, frowning once more over her toes showing below the hem of the *caftan*.

She had it on good authority that Zeineb Boudri was quite a bit taller than she was, and it had been confirmed by the over-long dresses she had been wearing for the past couple of days. Lisa found it curious, therefore, that a man as knowledgeable about women's clothes as Yusuf had shown himself to be should choose a *caftan* for his sister that would be much too short for her, but which fitted Lisa perfectly.

Catching sight of her reflection, she realised that she was smiling, and there was a bright glowing look in her eyes that made her shake her head as she turned away. Her fingers twirled the heavy silver bangle round and round on her wrist and she found she could remember with startling vividness, the light touch of Yusuf's fingers when he slid it over her hand.

Perhaps she would let him know that she had spotted his deception about the *caftan*, or perhaps not—not yet. In the meantime she was well satisfied with looking more exotic than she had ever done in her life before, in the richness of red and silver brocade; and more excited too at the prospect of a moonlight dinner with the donor.

CHAPTER SEVEN

YUSUF was standing by the rail when Lisa came on deck, and he turned at once when she appeared, almost as if he sensed her there, for he could surely not have heard the whispering softness of her sandalled feet on the deck. Seeing her, he flung the cigarette he was smoking over the side into the sea, and it struck her just how often she had seen him do that. It was a habit of his that she was getting used to, and it gave her a strange feeling of intimacy to realise it.

It had not occurred to her until she saw him that he would inevitably dress for the occasion too, and she felt her heart respond wildly at the sight of him. Tall and lean and so unmistakably masculine, he was an impressive man in any circumstances, but particularly so in the present ones, Lisa felt.

A white suit, possibly the same one she had seen him in the very first time their paths crossed, lent an added darkness to that stunningly sensual face, and a cream shirt and brown tie added a touch of formality. He appeared at ease, and yet somehow Lisa sensed a certain tension in him that could account for the slight upward angle of his chin as he regarded her steadily.

He studied her in that bold and uninhibited way that made her conscious of every curve of her body beneath the soft lines of the *caftan*, and of every movement she made as she crossed the deck towards him. Her legs trembled and felt almost too weak to support her suddenly, but she managed to smile confidently enough, 'Isn't it lovely?' She stood beside him at the rail, looking out across the unending ocean and the shimmering yellow path on its surface that flowed outward from the moon.

Yusuf said nothing in reply, but turned his head and smiled, showing gleaming white teeth in the dusky contours of his face, and a glowing blackness in his eyes. Distracted for a second by the appearance of Ali, he offered her his hand, leading her to where a table had been set on the narrow deck. Looking out over the sea, so that they seemed to be isolated from the rest of the world.

The food was in keeping with the idyllic setting, and although Lisa enjoyed it, she could not have described it in any detail, for her mind was in a kind of daze. Ali served them, quietly and discreetly as always, keeping their glasses filled with a light, sweet wine that seemed just right for an evening like this. But when he disappeared after serving them coffee, he left behind a curious sense of anticipation.

Too restive to bear the silence for long, Lisa held her glass pressed to her lips without drinking from it, and just avoided looking directly into the dark eyes that watched her so steadily. 'I feel so different in this dress,' she ventured breathlessly. 'It's so—so exotic.'

'It suits you perfectly.'

Lisa glanced at him from the concealment of her lashes, her eyes bright with mischief, and she could not resist a hint. 'And it fits me too,' she said, then laughed softly before taking a sip from her glass.

It would take more than that to put Yusuf at a disadvantage, she guessed, and he sat with his glass in one hand and the inevitable Kébir in the other; leaning back in his chair, confident and at ease. 'I like my women to look good,' he said, and the possessive note in his voice found a responsive chord in Lisa's heart, plucking it with skilful fingers.

She did not answer. The situation was too provocative,

and a shiver thrilled along her spine as she sipped more wine rather than look at him. Then some sound—some muffled, distant sound on shore reminded her that Zobi was just a few metres beyond where they were sitting in seeming isolation, and she remembered. Looking down at her hands, she clasped the wine glass in trembling fingers. It wasn't possible to forget Zobi completely, but she admitted to wishing she could, and that in itself was treachery enough.

'I hope nothing happens over there,' she said huskily, knowing he must have caught the sound too and been reminded. She glanced over her shoulder, although it was impossible to see anything from where they sat.

She half expected Yusuf to be angry about the reminder, but he merely looked thoughtful for a moment, then ground out the end of the Kébir in the ashtray, and took a sip from his glass, as if to give himself time to think about what he had to say. 'You know nothing about Zobi, do you, Lisa?'

She shook her head, more reluctant than she would have believed to have the fate of Zobi intrude into this perfect evening. 'You've told me I don't,' she reminded him. 'I'm no longer very sure of anything, to be quite honest. I know what we were told—that the whole village was to be razed to the ground to make way for a luxury hotel. Are you saying it isn't true?'

She found herself praying it wasn't true, even if it did make the whole protest pointless. But Yusuf was considering the question and taking his time about it. 'Basically it is true,' he allowed. 'Zobi is to be bulldozed to the ground and an hotel built on the spot.'

Raising her eyes, Lisa looked at him with mingled appeal and resignation. 'But?' she prompted.

'But it is not as—barbaric as you make it sound.'

'Destroying homes to make way for an hotel?' She

looked at him reproachfully. 'Oh, Yusuf, you don't really believe that, do you?'

'Most certainly I do,' he argued equably. 'Because I know it is true.'

As she watched him through her lashes, Lisa's emotions were oddly confused. She wanted to believe him, and yet if he was right the group, and herself, were horribly wrong; and she had the feeling that they were just that. 'Why don't you tell me where I—we're wrong?' she suggested.

He leaned his elbows on the table in front of him, which brought his face much closer, and made it much harder for Lisa to concentrate on what he had to say. The warmth of his nearness and that tantalising, familiar sensuousness teased her senses relentlessly, so that she trembled like a leaf while she sat with her eyes lowered, waiting for him to do as she suggested.

'Your whole objection is based on the fact that a village is to be demolished so that I can build my hotel, yes?'

Lisa nodded, but with a growing suspicion. 'You know what our objections are,' she told him, and he drew deeply on his cigarette before he went on.

'Yes, you have been quite explicit in your anger.' The fact that he smiled ruefully when he said it did not make Lisa feel any more confident. 'From the beginning your objection puzzled me,' he confessed, 'until I began to realise that you knew nothing about the situation at Zobi at all. Did you know that the village has been dying for many years now? The soil is arid, cropped until it is useless and unable to provide even a meagre living for its people.'

Lisa was looking at him with wide, uneasy eyes, and her heart was beating so hard it made her breathless. 'But we didn't know that—how could we?'

Just for a moment that hint of derision curled his lip,

and one black brow winged swiftly upward. 'It would have taken very little more effort to discover that than to discover my plans,' he told her.

'But—the people?' There was still that point to be considered, and she would not allow herself to overlook it. 'No matter how poor the living was, Zobi was their home and they're now without even a poor living, and their homes destroyed, or about to be.'

'You know that for certain?'

Lisa knew she had yet again reached the wrong conclusion, and her feelings were so confused that she found it hard to think clearly. By taking her, and the group's, case apart piece by piece, he was condemning her along with her friends, and yet she could not help feeling a wonderful sense of relief that he was proving to be less of a monster than they had made him out. She shook her head without saying anything, and Yusuf went on to enlighten her further, although it was a chastening experience as well as a pleasing one.

'My father has some land, quite close by Zobi, land that is richer and more fertile than Zobi has ever been, though further inland. The people lose their traditional home by the sea, but they gain a new village that is richer than anything they have ever known before. It is a fair exchange—we need the site on the ocean front, and the villagers need more fertile land to exist. Barter has long been our way of obtaining what we need, Lisa; the situation is not new to us.'

Lisa coped as best she could with the truth, but it was much too hard to suddenly do a complete about-turn on something she had felt so strongly about, and she sat for several moments trying to bring order to her chaotic thoughts. 'So—so no one's being driven out of their homes to make way for your hotel?'

Yusuf shook his head and took another cigarette. 'No.'

Watching the bright flame of the lighter make intriguing shadowplay on his face, Lisa felt curiously humble suddenly and she folded her hands together on the table to keep them from trembling so much. He reached over and folded one of his own big hands over hers, but when she would have told him how sorry she was, the touch of him disturbed her so much that she found it hard to say anything.

She tried hard to control the wildly erratic beat of her heart, but her head was spinning with excitement and relief, and she scarcely realised she was smiling. A small and very tentative smile, but one that gave her blue eyes a soft, misty look that was irresistibly appealing.

'It seems that I hardly know you at all,' she ventured in a small voice, and caught her breath when his long fingers squeezed hers hard for a moment. Almost afraid of saying anything that could spoil the moment, she hesitated before going on. 'Tell me,' she said softly, still with that misty look in her eyes. 'Tell me what you're really like, Yusuf.'

It was hard to say whether he minded being questioned, but Lisa took heart from the fact that his mouth still wore a faint half-smile and he did not let go her hands. 'First I want to know about you,' he insisted. 'You are an only child; am I correct?'

Lisa nodded, a slight angle to her chin defying him to agree with her suggestion. 'Which is probably why I'm spoiled.' He made no comment either way, so she went on, telling him the ordinary things like where she was born and where she went to school, and he seemed interested. 'My mother died a few years ago, and I lived with an aunt in England until last year, then I came out to join my father in Casa.' She raised her eyes that were big and shining but also vaguely defensive too. 'The rest you know!'

He was not looking directly at her any more, but down at the hand that clasped hers, and his fingers, she thought, tightened just a fraction when he spoke. 'And you have a boy-friend; this—Geoffrey Mason, eh?'

'I wouldn't exactly call him a boy-friend.' She tried to sound cool, but it was hard when those hard brown fingers were clasped so tightly over hers. 'I met him at a group meeting, the first I ever went to, and he——'

'Fell in love with you?' Yusuf suggested softly, then smiled and raised her hand to his lips. 'Yes, of course, he would.'

Lisa's heart pounded so hard it was difficult to hear even her own voice. 'I can't answer for Geoffrey,' she declared as firmly as her wavering voice was capable of being, 'but I'm certainly not in love with him. I—like Geoffrey, but that's all.' She looked at him for a moment steadily, because it suddenly seemed very important to convince him of that, but her lashes fluttered uneasily and it was hard to hold his gaze. 'Anyway, we've been through all this about Geoffrey and me, haven't we? Now I'd like to know about you.'

'Would you?'

His smile appeared to mock her curiosity, but his eyes were darkly serious, and she nodded firmly. 'Sheik Abahn's your—adopted father, isn't he?'

She had been about to say stepfather, but she had no wish to let him know that Ali had been talking to her about his family. 'My stepfather,' Yusuf confirmed. 'My true father was, as you seemed to know, a Frenchman, from Poitiers; a civil engineer, as I am, although I hardly knew him. His name was Joseph d'Acra, and of course you will already have recognised that I too have the same name translated into Arabic. My mother is a distant cousin of my—of Sheik Abahn's and she is now his second wife. They have a daughter, my sister Zeineb, who is about your age—very young.' He looked up briefly and smiled. 'But you will surely know all this from your dossier on me, eh?'

'I didn't have a dossier,' Lisa admitted, discomfited when she remembered how she had come by what little she knew of him in the beginning. 'We—just heard about you and what you were going to do, that was all. We—I didn't really know anything about you at all.'

'But now you feel that you do?'

She nodded, flicking the tip of her tongue across her lips in an unconsciously nervous gesture that he was sure to notice. 'I feel I understand you better.' She only very briefly raised her eyes and noticed he was smiling with his eyes now, too. 'I think I do.'

'For the sake of future relations, let us hope so, hmm?'

Something about the way he said it sent little shivers coursing along her spine, and Lisa hastily sought another subject. 'How long have you known my father?'

'Quite a long time; although it is my father who is better acquainted with him, in fact.'

Lisa pulled a face. 'And if I hadn't always discouraged Daddy from talking shop at home, I might have known all about you, and what——'

'An ogre I was?' Yusuf suggested softly.

'I didn't say that!' She denied it swiftly, but from the look in his eyes he knew it must have been close to the way she had thought of him initially. 'Not an ogre—I didn't say that.'

He got to his feet suddenly and reached for her hand, drawing her with him across to the rail, and for several minutes they stood just looking at the sea and the moon without saying a word, nor needing to. Then he turned and raised her hand in his, pressing his mouth to her open palm, his lips warm and startlingly evocative.

'So small and contrite because you misjudged me,' he whispered, and held her palm to the smooth tanned warmth of his cheek. 'So vulnerable and so—*charmante*, eh, Lisa?'

'Yusuf——'

She wasn't at all sure what she wanted to say, only that she was sorry she had believed what she had about him, and that she would try if she could to stop the group from making a terrible mistake. But it was so difficult to find the right words, and while she stood silently beside him, he leaned across and lightly kissed the soft skin below her ear, his smooth tanned cheek laid against hers for a second.

Turning her head but keeping her eyes hidden below their long brown lashes, Lisa tried hard to keep her racing heart under control. He was so close, much too close for comfort, and it was too easy to lift her face to him; to let herself lean towards him, sensing the tension in his lean hardness, and a reticence which she neither understood nor experienced herself.

With one hand she reached out and touched the soft silk shirt, feeling the warmth of his body through its fine texture and his heartbeat throbbing under her finger-tips, almost unaware of the gesture, but responding to a need to be in touch with him that could not be denied.

Then he took her hand in his again, his long fingers gentle as he twined them with hers, raising her hand to his lips again and pressing his mouth into her palm and then to his cheek. She was trembling but elated, and she did not recognise the emotions that surged through her, taking her breath away and setting up a wild, exultant beat in her heart, only responded to them eagerly.

'Lisa?' His voice shivered softly over her skin and she looked up. 'Will you do something for my sake, *petite?*' She nodded unhesitatingly and his eyes were glowingly dark when he looked down at her. 'Something you do not want to do?' Again she nodded willingly, ready to do anything he said. 'Will you please leave me now—go to your cabin, eh?'

Lisa caught her breath, and her fingers, still held by his, curled defensively. Her heart hammered and she was shaking with the shock of disillusionment as she stared at him, not wanting to believe it. 'You—you want me to go?'

He bent his head once more, to press his lips to her palm. 'It is not what I want, Lisa, it is what I remind myself I must do. I have promised your father that you are safe aboard the *Djenoun*.' He kissed her again, then turned the hand over and brushed her fingers with his mouth. 'Would you have me break my word?'

'Yusuf——'

'I cannot break my word,' he insisted, although he was obviously as reluctant as she was herself to bring the evening to such a disappointing end. Holding both her hands he pushed her away gently, watching her all the time with glowing dark eyes. 'Goodnight, Lisa,' he murmured quietly. 'Help me to keep my word.'

Lisa could see his predicament, and she wished she couldn't, but she was not going to be simply put off without some compensation and she dodged between those insistent hands suddenly, and put her hands on his shoulders. Standing on tiptoe, she lifted her mouth and kissed him lightly, almost teasingly, on the lips.

'Lisa!'

He reached out for her, but she was playing his game now, and she knew he would really hate to break his word to her father. Dodging his hands once more, she turned swiftly and hurried away from him. She turned when she reached the corner of the upper deck, and smiled at him, her eyes bright and gleaming in the soft light, the laughter of excitement hovering on her lips.

'Goodnight,' she said.

He would not follow her, she was almost sure of it, for he was a man of iron self-control as well as a man of his word. But she liked to think that he was tempted to do so, and as she walked along past the gangway she was still smiling to herself. How could she ever have guessed that dinner with Yusuf would end as it had? How could she have anticipated when she sneaked aboard the *Djenoun* that she would end by——

'Lisa!'

Startled out of her reverie, she took a moment to convince herself that she had actually heard the faint call, but she was almost sure she had. It seemed to have come from the shadows between the galley window and Yusuf's dining-salon, and she tried to see, narrowing her eyes against the shifting shadows. It would not be Yusuf, and Ali would never have used her first name so familiarly.

'Who is it?' She spoke in a whisper instinctively, without quite knowing why. Then someone emerged from the shadows and stepped into the light and she stared in startled disbelief. 'Geoffrey!'

'Sssh!'

He glanced over his shoulder and in her present state of mind it was all Lisa could do not to giggle at the suggestion of melodrama. He was dressed in dark clothes from head to foot, and he looked unfamiliar and vaguely sinister; his good-looking face as sober as she had ever seen it. He took a second or two to take in the different look that the red *caftan* gave her, then shook his head.

'I came to take you back,' he said in a harsh whisper. 'Come on, darling, while there's nobody about.'

'No, Geoffrey—I can't!'

He frowned, looking for a moment as if he did not believe his own ears. Only a few days ago Lisa would have welcomed his appearance as a chance to get away, but now she knew that if she went with Geoffrey Yusuf would never understand why. He would get quite the wrong idea, and that was what concerned her more than anything else at the moment.

'What do you mean, you can't?' he demanded hoarsely.

He held her wrist in a relentless grip and she realised how tensed up he must be. He had risked a great deal to come for her, and he was not going to understand her present state of mind unless she explained how wrong they had been about Yusuf and the Zobi project—how wrong they had been about the whole wretched business.

'Geoffrey, we've been wrong to blame Yusuf for Zobi.' She spoke quickly and in a small breathless voice, too anxious to convince him to realise why he narrowed his eyes as he did over her use of Yusuf's first name. 'We've got the wrong idea about——'

'What the hell has he been telling you?' he demanded, and Lisa hastily avoided his eyes.

'Only the truth,' she murmured huskily. 'Zobi isn't being vandalised, Geoffrey; it never was.'

'You believe that?' She nodded, desperate to convince him, and he eyed her with a strange coldness for a second or two. 'Because *he* told you?' he asked, and again she nodded agreement.

'I believe him, Geoffrey. He isn't at all like I—we thought. He does care about the people there, and he—they, Yusuf and his father, are doing something to help them.'

'My God!' Lisa had never seen that look in his eyes before, and she shrank from it, from the implications it made. 'It's time you went home,' he declared harshly. 'God knows what he's done to you, but he's got you eating out of his hand and talking like a fool. Now come on, Lisa, before it's too late!'

'No! No, I can't.'

Geoffrey did nothing for a moment, but he still had hold of her wrist and his grip did not relax at all. 'I haven't the time to hang about,' he said in a flat voice. 'Let's go!'

He tugged at her arm so suddenly that Lisa was half-dragged across to the gangway before she could resist, but when he would have pulled her down after him, she struggled, pulling back desperately. 'No, Geoffrey, wait!'

'What for?' he demanded in a harsh whisper. 'You've been conned, Lisa, and the sooner I get you away the better!'

Gripping her even more firmly he pulled at her arm again, while Lisa just as determinedly pulled back, and it wasn't until she won the tussle and her arm was free that she realised what the result was. She felt the silver bracelet slide down over her hand, cool and gleaming in the yacht's lights in the second before it disappeared into the darkness, then she heard the faint plop when it fell into the sea.

'It's gone! Oh, Geoffrey, my bracelet's gone!'

Her cry of despair was more anguished than she realised, and Geoffrey turned quickly to stare at her. 'Lisa, for God's sake, you'll bring the whole crew running!'

She didn't bother to correct him, but stared downward, trying to see into the dark water that lapped the sides of the *Djenoun*, and her eyes were filled with tears. His patience almost exhausted, Geoffrey made to take her arm again, but she avoided him, skirting round him and coming to a halt in the shadows of the deserted wheelhouse, defiant and unhappy at the loss of her precious bracelet.

'Are you mad?'

He dared not raise his voice, but he was angrier than Lisa had ever seen him and she recognised, even in her present mood, that he had cause to be. He had come to rescue her and she did not want to be rescued. Perhaps he was in love with her, as Yusuf had suggested, she had half suspected it before all this happened, but whether he was or not, she could not go off with him without saying a word to Yusuf—not now.

'Geoffrey, you have to tell them that there's no reason to stop what's going on at Zobi. It's all right, really, the people have been——'

'It's too late,' Geoffrey interrupted shortly. 'They're already in there, Lisa, and it doesn't take long to slit sacks of cement!'

She stared at him wildly; not so much concerned with what happened over there as with the possibility of Yusuf thinking she had had something to do with it. 'The crew are over there,' she whispered, and Geoffrey eyed her narrowly. 'Geoffrey, it isn't only the workmen on the site they'll have to get past, Yusuf sent the crew of the *Djenoun* over there too. They'll be waiting for them—oh, you must do something to stop them before it's too late!'

'It's already too late,' he said grimly. 'I told you—they're on the site and by now they're at work on the cement sacks. Nobody will see them, they're stacked at the far end under the trees.'

'Oh no!' She looked at him with eyes that were already filling with tears again. 'Yusuf will think——'

'Damn Yusuf!' Geoffrey snapped in a harsh whisper. 'We're getting out of here!'

He reached out for her again, but Lisa jerked her arm upward and out of his reach. The ensuing collision with something hard and painfully unyielding made her gasp aloud, but the worst was yet to come when she realised what she had come into contact with. There was a large brass bell hanging beside the wheelhouse and the blow she struck it with her forearm sent it swinging upwards, its clapper striking with ear-splitting resonance and repeating on the downward swing.

Geoffrey swore fervently, as stunned for a moment as she was by the sheer volume of sound, then he glanced over his shoulder. 'Someone's coming! Come on!'

He grabbed her roughly and this time Lisa was too dazed to resist when he hauled her across to the gangway and down the steep slope to the pier, scuttling like fugitives and bent almost double as they made for his car, parked at the end of the pier.

In normal circumstances he would never have got away with coming that close without being seen and challenged, but Yusuf had sent his entire crew across to Zobi, and Ali had been too busy to notice. Geoffrey opened the car door and bundled Lisa in, slamming the door shut almost before she was in the seat, then ran round and got in beside her.

The engine started up, splitting the quiet night like a scream, and he revved it up mercilessly, then put his foot down hard on the accelerator almost the moment they started moving. They shot away along the unlit sandy strip towards the highway in the second that Lisa recovered enough to see Yusuf and Ali come hurrying to the rail of the *Djenoun* and stand watching them go.

Bumping and bouncing along the track, Lisa sat with her head low, clinging to the side of the car and crying silently, as if her heart would break. Geoffrey said nothing but drove with his mouth set grimly, concentrating on the two blobs of light that danced in front of them, until suddenly he braked hard and leaned towards her to stare through the window beside her.

Distracted for a moment from her misery, Lisa too turned her head, and brushed blinding tears from her eyes so that she could see better. Lights moved erratically across the beach between Zobi and the *Djenoun*'s mooring, and even at that distance it was possible to make out the shadowy forms that carried them.

'That damned bell!' Geoffrey murmured harshly close to her ear, and laughed. 'The men on the site have gone to investigate; they think their boss is in trouble and they're going to his rescue!'

Lisa turned away, her hands tightly gripped in her lap, too unhappy to even cry any more. 'He'll never believe I didn't know you were going to be there, not now,' she said in a small flat, hopeless voice, and Geoffrey turned to frown at her impatiently as he started the engine again.

'Does it matter?' he demanded.

Lisa twisted her own restless fingers round and round her naked left wrist and the tears started again. 'Yes, it matters,' she said, but she doubted very much if he heard her.

CHAPTER EIGHT

LISA was aware that Madame Raymond was worrying about her and the fact that she had so little appetite since she came home, but she did not see what she could do about it. Whenever Lisa's father was away from home, Madame Raymond took upon herself the role of mother hen and fussed about everything she did. Normally she had very little to worry about, but now she eyed Lisa anxiously each time she shook her head over an enquiry if she was going out, or when meals went back only partly eaten.

Lisa had not been out of the house since she came home, but spent the time either reading or just sitting and doing nothing but feel sorry for herself. She was the first to admit that what had happened on board the *Djenoun* had changed her life in such a way that it would never be the same again.

Two days ago everything had seemed to be working out much better than she had dared hope, but now she was feeling more unhappy than she had ever been in her life before. She said little and smiled not at all, and her formerly healthy appetite had dwindled to almost nothing. And all because of a man who almost certainly would never wish to see or hear from her again.

She had telephoned her father and told him she was home, and thought it best in the circumstances to tell him everything that had happened after Geoffrey came on board the *Djenoun* that night—to rescue her, as he thought. It had hurt to realise that her father was less concerned when he learned that Yusuf was holding her aboard the *Djenoun* than he was about the manner of her parting from her erstwhile captor, and what had happened at Zobi.

He had told her that he considered handing out leaflets, as she and the rest of the group had done in the past, was not only foolish in the extreme, while they were guests in a foreign country, but discourteous too. As for scattering hundreds of bags of cement and then spraying the resultant mess with water, he could not find words to say how disgusted he was, and he had berated her soundly on the telephone for becoming involved with such people.

Lisa had hardly expected sympathy, but his stern condemnation of her, along with the actual participants in the act of vandalism, hurt. He would not, her father told her, get in touch with Yusuf ben Dacra and try to explain. She had got herself into the spot she was in through her own silly actions, and she could extricate herself as best she could. All he would do, if Yusuf should happen to be in touch, was to apologise on his own behalf for having such an irresponsible daughter.

Scolded by her father and wishing she had never heard of Balek!, Lisa had no idea what to do next. She could imagine Yusuf's fury at the unwarranted vandalism; and her driving away with Geoffrey as she had would make him see her as an accomplice. She should have struggled harder against his efforts to make her go ashore with him, she saw that now, but the clamour of that wretched bell had stunned her for the moment, and then Geoffrey's information that the group members were already concealed on the site and working havoc had completely robbed her of her senses.

She supposed she could not altogether blame Geoffrey, for she had been a willing enough participant in the scheme at the beginning, but yesterday when he had called she had refused to see him, and Madame Raymond had sent him away. Sooner or later, Lisa supposed, she would have to see him and talk with him, for Geoffrey was not the kind to give up easily.

At the moment she did not care if she never saw Geoffrey again, but it was hard to face the possibility of never seeing Yusuf any more, and she had shed tears about it in the privacy of her bedroom. Boy-friends had come and gone in the past, but not one of them had affected her in the same way as the tall autocratic man she had tracked down so determinedly, to deliver the group's warning.

He was so very different from any man she had known before. More mature, certainly, and more sophisticated; an intriguing mixture of arrogance and gentleness, and she would never be able to forget him. She had only to close her eyes and she was back on board the *Djenoun*, having dinner with him and listening avidly while he confided in her in a way she had never dared hope he would.

She could almost feel the touch of his fingers on her skin when he slid the silver bracelet on to her wrist; and remember how she had briefly thought it reminiscent of a shackle about her arm. Later she had laughed when he reminded her of his threat to put her in irons as a stowaway. Geoffrey, she believed, had lost her the bracelet and she almost hated him for it, even though it was unreasonable. The red *caftan* hanging upstairs in her wardrobe was the only thing she had to remind her of what she now saw as the most exciting days of her life.

Instinctively she turned her head when the salon door was opened, and Madame Raymond looked across at her enquiringly without coming in, her bright brown eyes anxious. 'Mr Mason is here again, Miss Pelham,' she told her. 'Will you see him today?'

It was an appeal, Lisa sensed, an appeal to return to normality, and she would very likely have agreed to see

Geoffrey anyway, but she was given no time to make up her mind. He appeared in the doorway behind the housekeeper, and there was an expression on his face that Lisa recognised. She could not face making an issue of whether or not she would see him, so she simply nodded assent, and Madame Raymond stepped aside to let him in.

'Lisa!'

Lisa could not understand why it should annoy her suddenly because he pronounced the 's' in her name as if it was a 'z', instead of giving it the same soft sibilance that Yusuf did. He came striding across the salon with an air of confidence that she immediately recognised was merely a cover for his nervousness. His eyes were sober, as they always were, but they were anxious too, and appealing in their way, and she reminded herself how warmly she would once have welcomed him. Sitting beside her on the cushion-piled ottoman, he took her hands in his, but after a moment Lisa eased them free.

'I came to see you yesterday,' he said, and she nodded.

'Yes, I know—Madame Raymond told me you'd been.'

'And you wouldn't see me?'

Lisa did not look at him, but smoothed out the skirt of her dress with restless hands. 'I didn't—I didn't feel like seeing anyone, Geoffrey.'

'Not even me? You're not ill, are you Lisa?' He was genuinely concerned for her, and Lisa wished she could feel more grateful for his concern, instead of vaguely irritated by it.

'No, of course I'm not ill, I'm just——'

She spread her hands helplessly, unable to describe the new and infinitely disturbing feeling she had, and Geoffrey tried to take them in his, but again she avoided him, trying not to look as if she was brushing him aside. 'You're disillusioned with what we're doing at Zobi?' he suggested quietly. His eyes searched her face, narrowed and hinting at impatience. 'I don't understand what's so different now to when you took it on yourself to tackle ben Dacra on his own territory, Lisa. What happened on board that damned yacht? You don't seem like the same girl!'

Lisa looked at him in silence for a moment, unwilling to tell him anything of what had happened aboard the *Djenoun* before he came and snatched her away. Also it angered her, perhaps unreasonably, that he was so unwilling to believe that Yusuf had told her the truth about Zobi. Why would he not believe that there was nothing to protest about, and never had been?

'Haven't you understood yet?' she said, and her voice suggested just how weary she was of trying to convince him. 'There was no need to do *anything* about Zobi. Sheik Abahn is rehousing the people in a new village, and on much more fertile land than they had at Zobi. They have a better life altogether than they had before, and they don't mind moving away—how could they in the circumstances? The soil at Zobi isn't fit for anything *but* building on, Geoffrey—if you really looked at it you'd see. You could have found out that as easily as you found out about Yusuf's plans to build an hotel there.'

It was quite unconscious when she quoted Yusuf's own argument, and she could see that Geoffrey was even more discomfited than she had been by the news. He did not want to believe it, she could see it in his face, and for a moment she almost pitied him, for he had been the prime mover in the Zobi project.

'You sound very sure of that,' he said after a moment or two, and Lisa frowned.

'You could discover how true it is by checking,' she challenged. 'Why don't you do that? You're the one who found out about the plan to build an hotel there, it shouldn't be beyond you!'

Lisa knew she was being unkind, cruel even, but she couldn't help herself. She felt sorry for him, although not in quite the same way she once had. It had been enough that he had risked his career for a worthwhile cause, but to realise that he had done so for a cause that did not even exist must be very hard to accept, and the bitterness of it showed on Geoffrey's good-looking features as he sat there trying to come to terms with reality.

'*You*'re obviously convinced anyway,' he said after a long silence, and Lisa nodded unhesitatingly.

'Yes, I am!' Clasping her hands tightly together, she looked down at them rather than at him. 'I think I know—I got to know Yusuf ben Dacra quite well being with him for those few days,' she said in a not quite steady voice, 'and I believe he told me the truth about Zobi. I'm absolutely certain he did.'

For several seconds Geoffrey's grey eyes speculated on just how well she had got to know her captor in those few days, but he did not ask her. Instead he shrugged his shoulders uneasily, and there was a downward droop to his mouth. 'What happens now?' he asked, and she knew he must be thinking about the effect of what the group had done at Zobi on his own future.

He hadn't been there personally, any more than she had herself, but the group would stand or fall in its entirety. She and Geoffrey would be counted as guilty as the ones who had actually vandalised the site, and the result could be disastrous to his career. The fact that he had gone into it knowing that would not make him feel any better about it, she guessed.

'Who knows what happens next?' she countered, and a short snatch of laughter ended breathlessly in something that sounded very much like a sob. 'It all depends on what Yusuf does, and in those circumstances I don't think I'll be much good as an advocate, although I'd try if I thought it would do any good.' She remembered

Yusuf's gentle hands and the warm exciting touch of his mouth, and closed her eyes tightly for a second when a thrill of pleasure ran through her. 'He isn't an unreasonable man when you know him,' she said, huskily unsteady. 'He's—he's——'

Her voice trailed off and she shook her head. Geoffrey was looking at her strangely, but she did not notice it for the moment. 'You *were* impressed,' he said with obvious dislike at the idea. 'You won't try to see him again, will you, Lisa?'

Taking a firm hold on her emotions, Lisa hesitated, although not for any doubt on her own part. 'I doubt if I'll have the opportunity,' she said quietly, then looked up again and met his eyes levelly. 'But whatever the circumstances, if I have the chance I'll take it. Because I *want* to see him again!'

'Oh, Lisa!'

She refused to avoid the reproachful look in his eyes, and shook her head, holding tightly to her self-control. 'I might have the chance—I don't know, but I know someone—I mean, I met someone once who might help.'

The idea of enlisting Yacub Boudri's help had only just occurred to her, but the more Lisa thought about that handsome and friendly younger brother of Yusuf's the more optimistic she felt. If he did not co-operate in this instance, of course, as he had on that first occasion, then she would be right back where she started, but it would surely do no harm to try.

'Yes, I think he might help.' She smiled, although it did not reach her eyes, and she did not attempt to enlighten Geoffrey about whose help she was hoping for. 'I can but try.'

'Lisa——'

'Please, Geoffrey, will you go now?' She interrupted him anxiously, for Geoffrey's pleading could well weaken her resolve and she needed all her tenacity at the moment. 'I have a lot to think about, and if I can get Yusuf to see me, to talk to me so that I can explain——'

Geoffrey looked as if he would have argued the point. He definitely did not like the idea of her trying to contact Yusuf again, that was clear, no matter what the cause. But Lisa was set on it now, and she waited impatiently for him to go, so that she could think of the best way of going about it.

'Don't worry,' she told Geoffrey, as she got to her feet. 'I know what I'm doing; I shan't go walking into the lion's den a second time, I promise you!'

'I hope not,' Geoffrey declared grimly, and as Lisa followed him to the door she echoed his sentiment even more fervently. She could not afford to make another mistake where Yusuf was concerned.

It was the following morning before Lisa finally made the decision to call on Yacub Boudri for help, and not altogether surprisingly, he proved much less difficult to contact than Yusuf had been in the initial stages of the group's campaign. Having got Madame Raymond to find the number for her, Lisa took the receiver over with visibly trembling hands, and asked if she might speak with Mr Yacub Boudri.

Similar requests when she had been trying to get in touch with Yusuf to deliver their warning had always met with a demand to know her business and whether or not she had an appointment. But she experienced no such difficulties in the case of his adopted brother. A male voice answered and merely asked to know who he should say was calling, but Lisa hesitated to tell him that at the moment.

'Would you tell him—will you please tell him it's the woman he met in the garden?' she said, and sensed the curiosity at the other end of the line.

'That is all?'

From the tone of the question Lisa suspected she was speaking to another of the Boudri brothers, and she moistened her dry lips anxiously before she answered. 'I—I think you'll find he understands,' she said, hoping she was not being too conceited, that Yacub Boudri had not forgotten all about her. 'If you'd ask him to speak to me, please, I think you'll find he'll come to the phone.'

'Oh, I am quite sure that he *will*!' the voice agreed readily, and Lisa was certain the man, whoever he was, was laughing to himself. 'If you will wait for just a moment, I will call him to the telephone.'

She murmured her thanks and, recalling Yacub Boudri's boldly flirtatious eyes, guessed that female callers were not at all unusual. It probably caused a great deal of good-humoured amusement among his married brothers. Although it was probably less usual for a caller to refuse to give her name and resort to a rather dramatic pseudonym.

She was banking a great deal on Yacub Boudri's co-operation, she realised as she waited anxiously at the end of the line, but he had proved that he had the ear of his older brother when he persuaded Yusuf to come out into the garden and see her that first evening, and she hoped he was not going to prove less helpful now.

Only seconds later she heaved a sigh of relief when he came on the line; his voice speaking its good but accented English, slightly curious but not unduly so. 'I remember that you are English and that you are very lovely,' he said when the preliminaries were dispensed with. 'But you are still a lady of mystery, it seems, yes? Will you not give me your name?'

'I'd rather not—it's rather difficult,' Lisa explained a little breathlessly. 'I prefer to speak first, Mr Boudri, if you don't mind, just for the moment.'

'As you wish, of course,' he agreed. 'But if you are seeking my assistance, as you did on the first occasion that we spoke together, I must insist that you call me

Yacub.' Lisa could imagine those velvet-dark eyes rolling expressively. 'But how may I help you, my dear young English lady? I hope this is not a request to see my brother again. It is very lowering for my ego, and not at all what I am accustomed to, being passed over in favour of Yusuf.'

Lisa was quite sure it wasn't what he was accustomed to, but she could tell from his voice that his ego was in little danger. 'As it happens,' she told him in a slightly unsteady voice, 'I *do* want to see Yusuf, but he won't want to see me, I know, and——'

'Ah, as I thought,' Yacub declared, obviously gratified with his own astuteness. 'You are Miss——'

'Please,' Lisa begged hastily. 'I don't want anyone to hear you; I don't want them to know you're talking to me.'

'Lisa Pelham, yes?' Yacub whispered into the telephone, and Lisa murmured agreement.

'You—you know about Zobi?'

He would know, of course, Lisa thought. She had decided the first time she saw him that Yacub Boudri was nobody's fool, for all he was a determined flirt and gave the impression of being too lighthearted to know about the business that his family were involved in. When he spoke again something in his voice suggested that he was much more on his guard now that he knew for certain who she was, and Lisa bit her lip anxiously.

'You wish to see my brother again?' he asked. 'In the circumstances it will not be easy, as I am sure you will realise, Miss—*mademoiselle*.'

'I know.' Her voice caught in her throat, and she sounded so obviously unhappy that even a less susceptible man than Yacub Boudri would have been touched. 'I realise that he's still down at Zobi, but if I go down there, he won't——'

'No, no, my dear Miss Pelham!' She hesitated, plainly

confused, and Yacub Boudri went on. 'My brother is no longer at Zobi, he returned here to Casablanca yesterday, by car. The *Djenoun* was too slow, so he said, although I have never known him think so before.'

Why else would he want to return to Casablanca so quickly, Lisa thought, unless it was to consult with his solicitors about what action to take against the group and, inevitably, against herself as a member of the group? If he had been so quick to seek revenge then perhaps she was wasting her time trying to reason with him. Her heart was thudding hard and making her head pound so that she could not think very clearly.

'I—I didn't know that,' she said in what was barely more than a whisper, and tried to decide what to do next. 'Do you know—I mean have you any idea why he came back so soon?' She knew she had overstepped the mark there, and hastened to recoup her position if she could. 'No, I'm sorry, Mr Boudri, I can't ask you that. I'm sorry.'

'I could tell you very little, even if I were at liberty to say what the position is, my dear lady,' he told her, and Lisa accepted the softness of his voice as a sign of sympathy.

He made no other move, offered no solution, but at least he had not so far dismissed her out of hand, and she took heart once more. 'It is very important that I see Yusuf—your brother,' she stressed, huskily anxious.

'That is what you told me on that first occasion, if I remember,' he reminded her, but something about the way he said it suggested he was already weakening.

'It's true,' she vowed. 'It really *is* important to a lot of people, including my father.'

'John Pelham?' Obviously he too knew her father, and he would realise well enough just what her involvement with Balek! could mean to him if Yusuf took legal action against the group. 'It is a most unfortunate situation and I feel for——' Lisa heard him heave a great sigh, and she could imagine his expressive hands spread in resignation. 'Very well, if you wish to try and talk to my brother about it, I will do what I can to arrange a meeting between you. I have a great respect for John Pelham, and I dislike seeing lovely women weep. I will help you if I am able.'

'Oh, thank you, thank you!' Lisa almost wept in her relief, and at the other end of the line Yacub Boudri made soft clucking sounds of consolation.

'Do you know the café called La Place, on Rue Hassan?' he asked, and Lisa murmured agreement.

'Yes, I know it.' It was not the whole truth, but she would soon find the café if it meant she might see Yusuf again.

'If you will be there at one half-hour past one o'clock,' he went on, 'I will do my best to see that Yusuf is there with me. I cannot promise anything; you will understand that—my brother is not the man he once was, Miss Pelham, and I have a curious inclination to believe that you are in some way responsible for that.'

Lisa's heart sank, but she was not ready to give in yet, and she moistened her lips anxiously before she spoke. 'Did—did he blame me for what happened?'

'He has said very little about what happened,' Yacub told her very seriously. 'But I have never before heard Yusuf curse the fickleness of the feminine character as he has since he returned from Zobi, and since you were the only woman on board his yacht and you apparently fled from it so dramatically, I am forced to believe that you are the particular woman against whom he raves.'

'I'm sorry.'

There seemed little else to say, for she felt very close to tears at the moment. But Yacub Boudri seemed to be taking it all in his stride. 'Then you should tell him so when you meet, my dear Miss Pelham. The café is small and quiet—very discreet, an ideal place for a rendezvous. All that you need to do is to be there, do you understand?'

'Oh yes, I understand, I understand perfectly, and I'll be there!' Too excited and relieved to think clearly, Lisa laughed, making her feelings all too plain to the listener. 'I don't know how to thank you, Mr Boudri; I'm so grateful to you for helping when you don't know me.'

A soft and very suggestive chuckle bubbled against her ear. 'That is something that can be remedied, perhaps,' he suggested. 'I will see you again at half-past one o'clock, eh? Goodbye, Lisa!'

Lisa found the café without too much trouble, but she hesitated for some time about going in. She had never felt more nervous and panicky in her life, and the thought of seeing Yusuf again gave rise to so many different emotions that her head was spinning. Twice she started to go inside and each time she retreated, until finally she reminded herself that Yacub Boudri had probably had a great deal of difficulty persuading his brother to accompany him, and that he had arranged the meeting at her request.

Last-minute fears that he had not been able to persuade him after all were banished the moment she walked in through the door, for she spotted them right away, catching her breath at the sight of Yusuf's dark head. He sat facing Yacub across one of the small tables and he had his back to her as she crossed the floor, but her senses responded urgently, demolishing the last remnants of her self-possession.

Yacub was chattering animatedly, the menu in his hand, but Yusuf appeared to be paying very little attention to what he said. Even from the back he seemed to have a distant, thoughtful air about him, and as she approached their table Lisa almost panicked once more and turned away. But Yacub had seen her, and he was already on his feet, a wide welcoming smile seeking to reassure her.

Yusuf rose too, automatically polite whatever he thought of her personally, and her heart skipped wildly when he seemed to tower over her suddenly. 'Ah!' Yacub Boudri said with a convincing show of surprise that Lisa would have been fooled by it if she had not known better. 'I remember—you are the lovely lady whom I found hiding in my father's garden one evening, are you not? How could I forget so charming an intruder?' He extended a hand and when Lisa placed hers into it, he immediately turned it over and conveyed it to his lips. 'Do you remember me, dear lady?'

'Oh yes. Yes, of course.' Lisa licked anxiously dry lips and tried to smile, but she was too aware of that other tall, glowering figure beside her, and her hand trembled. 'Mr Boudri—Mr Yacub Boudri.'

'You know my brother, of course?' He skimmed over the formalities and invited her to sit with them. 'I did not know on that occasion that your father was John Pelham.' Lisa nodded, not yet accepting the invitation to sit down. 'Please sit down and join us, Miss Pelham, will you? Will you allow me to buy you lunch?'

It was not a situation that a man of his nationality would have staged normally, and certainly he would not have approached a strange woman, and a foreigner, so boldly. But Lisa had come to the conclusion that Sheik Abahn's youngest son was a law unto himself, especially where women were concerned. In the circumstances there was little she could do but take the invitation at its face value, and she sat down, though she carefully avoided Yusuf's sternly suspicious gaze.

She hesitated about taking the menu from her beaming host, too intent on Yusuf's reaction to take notice of anything but him for the moment. He was so close that she could have reached out and touched him, but unlike Yacub he did not sit down again. Instead he remained on his feet, standing behind the chair he had occupied, with his big hands curved tightly over the back. He addressed himself to his brother, quietly but with an obvious dislike of the situation he found himself in, and Lisa knew he had not been fooled by Yacub's strategy, however convincing it had seemed.

'I agreed to have lunch with you because you disliked eating alone,' he told Yacub in his deep and perfectly controlled voice. 'Now that you have found yourself a companion I will return to the work I interrupted to come with you, Yacub. I am sure you will excuse me in the circumstances.'

'Oh, but in such charming company, surely you will stay,' Yacub insisted.

But if Yacub really believed he might persuade him, Lisa knew better. Perhaps she had more often been on the receiving end of Yusuf ben Dacra's disapproval than his younger brother had, and recognised the signs more readily. She had never felt more unhappy in her life, although she tried hard not to let it show, keeping her eyes downcast to hide the hurt she felt.

The familiar warmth of his nearness played on her senses as it always did, and when he moved, his sleeve brushed her shoulder, setting her heart racing wildly. She felt she would never be able to come close to him without feeling as she did now, and in the circumstances she despaired of ever being able to forget him. He was turning down his brother's invitation not, she felt sure, because he had important work to occupy him, but because he would rather do anything than sit down to another meal with her.

'Yusuf.' She ventured his name, but dared not look at him yet, and her heart hammered urgently as she sought for words that would convince him. 'Please believe me,

I—I didn't want to go with Geoffrey——'

'I am to believe that? When you wasted so little time, after he came for you?' he interrupted harshly. 'And ringing the bell to let your friends know that you were safely freed from my clutches and they could go ahead with their destruction—whose idea was that, *mademoiselle*? Yours or your—friend's?'

'Neither!' Lisa denied, breathlessly anxious. 'I didn't know Geoffrey was coming, and I hit the bell by accident! It *wasn't* a signal!'

'But it triggered off the attack on the site,' Yusuf said, relentlessly pressing home his point. 'And you cannot have struggled for very long against your rescuer since you were already in his car and driving away when I arrived to see what had happened.'

'But I *did* try to get away from him!'

'Why?' Yusuf demanded remorselessly. 'Your father told me that you have been seeing the man for some time, and you warned me often enough that he, or someone, would be coming to take you back! Why deny that he is your lover simply to try and convince me? Or do you think me a complete fool because I allowed myself to be—pleasant to you?' Lisa noticed how tightly the big hands were on the back of the chair, and shivered. 'Perhaps you do have reason to believe me a fool,' he allowed in a harsh flat voice, 'but no longer, Miss Pelham, I promise you!'

Lisa glanced up, suddenly understanding, she thought. Yusuf ben Dacra would not forgive easily, but especially he would not forgive someone whom he had allowed to see the softer, more gentle side of his character. But Yucub was clearly in the dark, shaken by the virulence of his brother's anger, and he attempted to soothe the situation without yet knowing the cause of its violence.

'Yusuf, please,' he said, and a wary kind of smile hovered about his mouth. 'I am sure you do Miss Pelham an injustice. You are angry——'

'And with good cause, as Miss Pelham well knows!' Yusuf told him impatiently.

'But surely,' Yacub ventured a second attempt, 'you should listen to what Miss Pelham has to say.'

'Oh, please!' Lisa's voice choked in her throat and she could only shake her head for several seconds before she recovered enough to go on. 'It's no good, Mr Boudri, Yusuf—your brother's made up his mind and he isn't going to change it on my account!'

Yusuf still stood with his hands on the back of the chair, and the waiter had been deterred enough by his expression and his obvious anger not to approach them so far. Catching his eye, Yacub shook his head slightly, then once more looked up at his brother. But he was given no time to say anything more; Yusuf was still very firmly in charge of the situation.

'I have a great deal of work to be done,' he said, once more addressing himself to his brother. 'If you will excuse me, Yacub; I am sure that Miss Pelham will find it less embarrassing if I leave you.'

'You are determined?' Yacub was not accustomed to being on the losing side either. 'Yusuf——'

'Please excuse me! *Mademoiselle!*'

He inclined his arrogant head with chilling politeness and Lisa watched him go stalking back the way he had come, with her hands pressed tightly on the table top. No one said anything until that tall, autocratic figure had disappeared from view, then Yacub turned and looked at her, his handsome features distorted by a grimace.

'What can I say?' he pleaded, and was obviously at a loss to understand his brother's lack of co-operation. 'I had not thought he would behave so, Miss Pelham, and I do not pretend to understand him in his present mood.'

Unwilling to condemn him out of hand, for all his stubbornness, Lisa offered excuses for him. 'I can see why he's so angry,' she said, and Yacub Boudri was bound to notice how small and unsteady her voice was. 'I—I just wish he'd given me the opportunity to explain *my* part in it—or my innocence of taking any part at all.'

'You knew nothing of what they did—those others?' Lisa shook her head, and Yacub's dark eyes narrowed shrewdly. Leaning his elbows on the table in front of him, he looked at her for a moment, then half-smiled. 'Then he must be convinced of it,' he declared.

Lisa was shaking her head, her eyes brimming with unshed tears, and her voice was barely more than a husky whisper as she put down the menu unread; she couldn't eat anything, it would choke her at the moment. 'He won't listen,' she guessed. 'I know him—he won't listen once he's made up his mind.'

'You *know* him?' Yacub Boudri reached for her hand and raised it to his lips, leaning towards her and watching her with those velvety dark eyes. 'Not as well as I do, I think, my dear Lisa. I shall arrange for you two to meet again, and this time you will make him listen to you. Oh yes, you *can* make him listen,' he insisted when she would have denied it. He raised her fingers and kissed them lightly, his smile wide and confident once more. 'I am not a gambling man,' he told her, 'but I would wager many *dirhams* that in the right circumstances you could make my brother Yusuf do almost anything you wished.'

Lisa gave him a small and very uncertain smile, but said nothing. She had her hands held very tightly together on the table, and in her heart she prayed that he was right. She could not bear to think of Yusuf going on thinking she had lied to him—she did not for the moment even remember that her father and Geoffrey had a lot at stake too. Only that she had to convince Yusuf that he was wrong about her part in it.

CHAPTER NINE

For three days now Lisa had been waiting for something to happen, and so far nothing had. Yacub Boudri had promised that he would do something about arranging another meeting with Yusuf, but after the reception of his last effort, she was doubtful if he could manage another, no matter how willing he was to help.

She had not seen Geoffrey since her last meeting with Yusuf either, but when Madame Raymond told her that he was there to see her, she shrugged resignedly and said to let him come in. While she waited she made a determined effort to look less woebegone than she felt, although her smile definitely looked strained, and her caller did not miss the fact.

'Hello, Lisa.' He looked as if he was about to take her hands, thought better of it, and sat down in one of the armchairs instead of on the ottoman beside her as he would normally have done, although Lisa was too distracted to notice at the moment. 'I—I hope you're O.K.,' he ventured, and she nodded.

'Yes, thank you.'

'I haven't been again, because——' He shrugged uneasily and did not look at her but down at the floor between his feet. 'I had the feeling last time I was here that you more blamed me for getting you off ben Dacra's yacht than looked on it as a rescue.'

Lisa shook her head. It was difficult to know just how honest to be with him, for she had never felt so distant from Geoffrey before, and it made her uneasy. 'I didn't need rescuing, Geoffrey; my father knew where I was, he's known the Sheik's family for years although I didn't know it, and I wasn't exactly a prisoner on the *Djenoun.*'

'So I noticed.' His grey eyes met hers, remembering and resenting the glamorous red *caftan* she had been wearing, and the way she had been smiling to herself as she came along the deck. 'I've realised since that you were probably enjoying yourself—sorry I broke it up!'

He was bitter, and Lisa could not really blame him. He had been so sure that she was a miserable captive of the man they had all decided was some kind of monster, when in fact nothing was further from the truth. Particularly at that moment when she had just left Yusuf's arms, thrilling with the warm excitement of his kiss. She avoided Geoffrey's eyes again, her hands in her lap and the fingers of one hand encircling the other wrist; and Geoffrey noticed that too.

'I'm sorry about the bracelet too,' he said in a flat cool voice. 'I gathered you set some store by it, although I don't remember seeing you wear it before.'

'Yusuf bought it for me in Goulimine.'

'In Gou——? You went to——' He stopped, frowning darkly, and his face looked faintly flushed. 'I *have* been a fool, haven't I?'

Lisa was too hurt herself not to appreciate his feelings and she looked across at him anxiously. 'Oh no, Geoffrey, not a fool, I won't allow that! You took a chance, coming for me as you did, but if only you'd let me explain what was actually happening at Zobi when I tried to, I shouldn't be feeling quite so wretched.'

'Like I said,' Geoffrey insisted bitterly, 'I was a fool!' They were silent for several moments, then he looked across at her again, his eyes questioning. 'What happens now, Lisa? Was your—your contact any use to you? Could he help?'

Lisa got up and paced restlessly about the room while she talked, wishing she knew just how much Yacub Boudri was able to do for her. 'He tried,' she told

Geoffrey, 'but the meeting was a dismal flop; Yusuf wouldn't listen to me. He's promised to arrange another meeting, but—I don't know. I honestly don't see what he can do if Yusuf goes on digging in his heels.' She jerked her hands impatiently and frowned. 'Oh, why is he so stubborn? Why won't he let me explain that I didn't know about the wretched raid on the village?'

Geoffrey pressed his fingertips together and studied the resultant steeple thoughtfully, his mouth set firmly into a straight line. 'It matters to you, doesn't it?' he asked. 'It matters to you that he thinks you knew about what the group were doing in the village?'

Lisa nodded. 'Yes,' she admitted after a second or two, 'it matters to me.'

The grey eyes were raised and met hers squarely, and there was something in them that showed such hurt, Lisa flinched from it. 'I was afraid so,' Geoffrey said quietly.

'Oh, Geoffrey——' She looked across at him and her mouth trembled. She could think of nothing else to say at the moment, but she knew he hurt in the same way as she did herself, and she wished she was not so sure of the reason.

'You know how I feel about you,' Geoffrey said in a quiet, steady voice that affected her dangerously. 'Maybe I should have said something sooner, but I thought you knew.' Briefly his solemn features softened into a rueful smile. 'The reticent Englishman, I suppose,' he suggested. 'I took it for granted it would work out, and I didn't take into account the effect that men like ben Dacra can have on a woman.'

Lisa had never before been in such a situation, and she felt too unsure of herself, too vulnerable, having it spelled out to her as Geoffrey was doing. It was like losing both of them in a way, and she felt horribly close to tears when she realised it. She had little hope that Yusuf would relent, and she could never again be on quite the same easy footing with Geoffrey after this moment.

'Would you rather I went?'

Geoffrey's voice dragged her back to immediate decisions, and she looked up quickly, unsure if she wanted him to go or not. 'I suppose it might be better,' she agreed in a small wistful voice. 'Somehow I feel——' When she realised there were tears in her eyes she brushed them away with the back of a hand. 'I'm sorry, Geoffrey, I—I'm not unaffected by——' She swallowed hard. 'I didn't want you to fall in love with me,' she told him huskily. 'I—I know how it can hurt.'

'Oh, Lisa, Lisa!' He did not take her in his arms, but put his hands on her shoulders and pressed his fingers into her flesh with a fierce tautness, while he looked down at her unhappy face. 'If that—that damned Sheik of Araby of yours doesn't melt at the sight of you, he isn't worthy of his French father! He won't be able to forget you, not if he's anything of a man!' He bent his head and lightly kissed her mouth. 'I know I never will,' he whispered. 'Goodbye, my love!' He kissed her once more, then turned and was gone.

John Pelham was due home the following day, and Lisa was not looking forward to meeting her father face to face in the present circumstances. He had telephoned once more since that first angry message, and been a little more understanding, but having to explain the whole situation to him in person was not something she looked forward to.

She was flicking through a magazine and not really seeing anything at all, when she received a telephone call from Yacub, and at the sound of his voice she felt a sudden surge of hope. He was as charming as ever and sounded so cheerful that she could not think otherwise than that he had some news for her.

'There will be a dinner party at my father's house this evening, my dear Lisa,' Yacub informed her, his voice discreetly lowered. 'I hope that you will be here.'

Lisa tried to think clearly, but found it impossible. How could he expect her to simply arrive at his father's house as a guest? He surely must see that it wasn't possible. 'Yacub, I can't—I mean, I couldn't come to the house, not after last time. I doubt if I'd be admitted.'

'You were admitted once before,' Yacub reminded her, and laughed softly, so that there was no mistaking his meaning.

'You mean I should come in by the—— Oh no, I couldn't! Not again, I wouldn't dare!'

'Not even to see Yusuf again?' Yacub dangled the bait tantalisingly, knowing she would find it hard to resist, but Lisa took her time.

Her fingers curled tightly around the receiver, and her teeth gnawed anxiously at her lower lip while she considered the idea. It was a temptation, and she was ready to go, but it was surely taking an awful chance to give Yusuf the opportunity of once more forcibly removing her from his father's property.

'Lisa?' Yacub's voice recalled her and she blinked herself back to alertness.

'Are you sure, Yacub? I mean—the last time I came in through that way he threw me out into the street.'

Yacub clucked his tongue in disgust at such folly, but he still sounded brightly optimistic when he spoke again. 'But that was before he had spent several days—and nights—on board the *Djenoun* with you, lovely Lisa, was it not?' He chuckled, as if the subterfuge amused him. 'You come to the small gate as you did before,' he told her, 'and I will make certain that it is open for you. Then you wait in the garden, just as before, eh? Yusuf will come to you, I promise!' He seemed to sense her hesitation and clucked his tongue reprovingly. 'Trust me, eh?'

'Yes. Yes, of course,' Lisa said. There was nothing else she could do, she knew, for she could not resist such a chance; it might never occur again. 'I'll be there,' she said. 'And—thank you, Yacub.'

Madame Raymond looked pleased when Lisa came downstairs, obviously dressed for an evening out, although she was probably puzzled by the fact that Geoffrey was not there to collect her. Instead a taxi came for her and whisked her through the same route that she and Geoffrey had taken that evening that now seemed so long ago.

Some unconscious superstition had made her pass over a yellow dress in her wardrobe; she had worn a yellow dress the last time she went to Sheik Abahn's house, and it had scarcely proved a lucky choice. Instead she put on the red *caftan* that Yusuf had bought for her, and looking at her reflection, felt a curious fluttering sense of excitement when she recalled the last occasion on which she had worn it.

Not that she anticipated anything half so pleasant happening this evening, but there was something very special about the richness of the red brocade, and she knew that whatever happened, no other dress would ever mean quite so much to her. It represented a moment in her life when she had been quite idyllically happy for a short time.

The taxi turned into the same narrow and dimly lit street whose high walls reminded her of a prison, and she shivered again at the illusion, keeping a sharp lookout for one particular small gate set in the secretive blankness of the walls. The driver looked at her with undisguised curiosity when she asked to be set down about halfway along the street, and he seemed to be questioning the wisdom of her decision, using both Arabic and French to tell her his opinion, neither of which she understood.

He was concerned, she supposed, at the idea of leaving her there alone in that dark, deserted street, but Lisa gave him a reassuring smile and waited until he had driven off once more, in the direction of the more brightly lit streets of the town, before she ventured to try the little gate in the wall. Just as she had on that first occasion, she took a moment to gather her courage, although this time she knew what to expect when she opened it, and prayed only that Yacub Boudri had made certain the gate was unlocked.

The long dark passageway smelled dank and cold, as it had before, and she shivered involuntarily as she drew her skirts close about her, listening to her own ghostly footsteps whispering over the hard ground. She was trembling violently and just before she reached the end of the passage, she paused to try and gain control of her emotions.

The scents of the garden, and particularly of the big magnolia that grew by the entrance of the passage, were sweet and heady as she stood drawing in deep uneven breaths, to try and steady her thudding heart. If it didn't work; if Yusuf still refused to let her explain, she vowed she would leave Casablanca and never come back. Her father would probably not understand her reasons, but Geoffrey would, she knew, and she spared a moment to wish things could have been different between her and Geoffrey. Yusuf ben Dacra was an impossible dream and she would have been much wiser to have settled for what Geoffrey had to offer.

She could hear voices from the house, and see lights beaming out on to the patio and the garden. Everything seemed so much the same as it had been on that first occasion that she could almost believe she had dreamed everything in between. As she moved out of the shelter of the passage, the outer leaves of the magnolia brushed her cheek with their cool touch as she passed, and she stood for a moment looking across at the lighted room full of people.

The fountain playing into the big stone basin had a curiously soothing effect, she found, and she walked over to it without thinking, reaching down to dabble her fingertips in the cool water while she tried to bring order to her chaotic senses, afraid that Yusuf would not come, and almost as fearful of what might happen if he did.

Behind her the reflection of a huge jacaranda fluttered its fernlike leaves across the light of a dying moon in a deep purple sky, while her own reflection shimmered palely in front of it. Idyllic and peaceful, it seemed like a million miles from the violence and anger that had brought her back there, and inevitably her thoughts turned to Yusuf.

To the thrill of his nearness on a moonlit deck, and the caress of his strong fingers on her skin, his lips lightly pressed to her neck while he pleaded with her to take away the temptation of her closeness so that he would not break his word to her father. Her own happy laughter in the moment before Geoffrey appeared and put an end to her happiness.

She caught her breath sharply and spun round when another, taller and darker, reflection appeared behind her own, watching her with eyes as dark and gleaming as jet. A lean, tanned face that seemed to be carved from teak and looked just as hard and unyielding; duskily dark against a white shirt, and a cream suit that skimmed the panther-lean lines of his body.

Lisa's eyes were wary. Her hands gripped the edge of the stone basin and were shaking so much that she felt sure he must notice. She shook her head slowly, bereft of speech, and able to do no more than murmur his name with the soft uncertainty of an appeal. 'Yusuf.'

'I have been persuaded to see you against my better judgment.' The harshness of the words spoken in that deep and incredibly affecting voice brought a mixed reaction from her. She supposed it could be considered an encouraging sign that he had come out to see her, at least.

'It's—it's good of you to see me,' she whispered, and wondered what had happened to that defiant and liberated woman who had stormed the *Djenoun* in her determination to pass on the group's warning about Zobi.

He made a sound with his mouth that seemed to suggest he was as impatient with his own weakness as with her, and reached into a pocket for one of the long black Kébirs he smoked. Lisa watched the lighter flame dance tiny shadows across the so familiar lines of his face and felt as if her legs had turned to water. How was it possible to love a man so much in so short a time, and when his interests seemed destined to clash with her own?

'Will you listen to me, Yusuf?' she asked in a small soft voice.

He sat himself down on the edge of the stone basin with a sudden and unexpected movement that made her start visibly, and Yusuf eyed her for a second through the smoke from his cigarette. 'I have promised that I will listen to you,' he said. 'My brother seems to think I have ill-used you, and that I should—unbend a little. Those are his words, not mine,' he hastened to add, and Lisa thanked heaven for Yacub's determination.

She was so actutely conscious of him as a man that it was hard to think of anything but the excitement of being close to him again, and of the gentleness she knew those big hands were capable of. Her legs trembled alarmingly, and she knew he had noticed the red *caftan* the moment he saw her. He probably suspected her motive for wearing it, but to Lisa it was a kind of talisman, and she placed her hands flat against her thighs as she faced him, smoothing the rich soft brocade with her palms.

'There was no other way of getting to see you,' she told him huskily. 'I hope you won't blame Yacub for helping me.'

'For letting you in through the rear entrance; the way you came in the last time,' he remembered, and she watched him anxiously.

'Not quite like last time,' Lisa denied. 'Yacub had nothing to do with last time.'

Yusuf looked at her steadily. He appeared to be relaxed, sitting on the edge of the fountain with one leg swinging carelessly, but there were taut little lines at the corners of his mouth that showed just how tense he was in reality. 'Tell me,' he said quietly. 'Tell me what it is I came here to listen to.'

He sounded so much as if he had already made up his mind, as if he was so sure she could not prove herself innocent of what had happened at Zobi, that her eyes filled with tears suddenly. 'Oh, Yusuf, don't judge me so harshly!' She made the plea in a voice that was no more than a whisper, and looked at him appealingly. 'I didn't know what was going to happen, don't you realise that I couldn't have? Do you think I could have lied to you so—so boldly?'

He looked no less forbidding, but as so often happened, it was his voice that told her he was weakening slightly. 'I would hope not,' he said, and Lisa took hope from it, watching him anxiously.

'I *couldn't*,' she insisted. 'Whatever you think of me, Yusuf, I've never lied to you. I *didn't* know that the rest of them were there, not until Geoffrey told me, and then I wanted to come and tell you, to warn you. I wanted Geoffrey to stop them, I tried to make him understand, but there was such a—a confliction of purposes, I was confused. Geoffrey was only interested in getting me away from the *Djenoun*, whether I wanted to go or not.'

'And you went with him.'

'I had no choice,' Lisa insisted despairingly. 'I was upset because I'd lost my bracelet overboard and I blamed Geoffrey; then he told me about the group and I wanted to come and tell you. He pulled one way and I tried to pull away from him, it was all so—so quick. Then that blessed bell—I caught it with my arm when I was trying to keep out of Geoffrey's reach. It frightened me half to death when it made that din, and before I realised what was happening, I was being hauled down the gangway and pushed into his car. He was so—angry I couldn't reason with him.'

Yusuf looked at the tip of his cigarette and his eyes were hidden by the thick blackness of his lashes. 'He was jealous, of course,' he said without troubling to make it a question, and Lisa was in no mind to deny it.

'Yes, he was.'

'He is in love with you?'

He still did not look at her, and once again Lisa answered him without prevarication. 'He says he is.'

'Then of course he was jealous.'

He looked at her for a moment in a way that made her remember her laughter, only seconds before Geoffrey came on the scene, and the reason for her glowing happiness. When he stood up he threw the end of the Kébir into the fountain and to Lisa the gesture was achingly familiar as she watched the tiny red spark die in the tinkling water. He looked down at her, tall and disturbingly close, so that she could almost touch the lean body and feel the warmth of him on her own soft skin.

'Had he reason to be, Lisa?' he asked softly, and she did not answer quite so readily this time.

She was shaking like a leaf, and her hands trembled

even when she held them close together in front of her. 'I wish I knew,' she whispered.

'Why did you come, Lisa?'

She gathered her thoughts hastily into some kind of order, and remembered at last that she was there also to plead for her father and for Geoffrey and the rest. It had been so easy to forget them in the past few minutes. 'I wanted to ask you—I had to plead with you not to—to take revenge on the others.' Her voice wavered and almost broke, but he offered no support, no help. 'My father will suffer if you take legal action,' she went on, softly, breathlessly, her voice as unsteady as the legs that barely supported her. 'I don't like to think—I hate to think of you being vengeful when it can hurt so many people. Not just the ones who've been thoughtless and —and silly, but my father too, and other families.'

'And you came to plead with me for them?'

Lisa made no bones about it. She lifted her eyes and looked at him. 'Yes,' she said.

He stood for several minutes, saying nothing, with his black brows just slightly drawn, his eyes hidden by those thick lashes again. 'Just this once,' he said after what seemed like an eternity, and Lisa let out her breath in a long shivering sigh. 'This once only.'

Reaching up she put her hands either side of his head, then tiptoed to kiss his cheek. 'Thank you,' she whispered huskily. 'Thank you, Yusuf!'

The touch of those strong brown fingers on her bare arms evoked sensations she could do nothing to control, and she was drawn against the warm vigour of his body with a slowness that was somehow breathtakingly sensuous. 'Was that the only reason you came?' He asked the question softly as his arms tightened about her, and Lisa shook her head.

'No,' she whispered. His lips brushed her cheek lightly, coaxingly, and her heart expanded like a flower in the warm sun, beating so hard that it throbbed in her brain like a drum. 'I—I wanted to see you again; I wanted to—be near you, to——'

She caught her breath; so sure of her own feelings, but not yet sure enough of his to go on. Without a word he brought his dark, shadowed face down to hers and sought her mouth with soft, gentle kisses that promised so much more. Then the gentleness was gone suddenly and she was swept against him with a fierce fury of passion that snatched the breath from her body, and kissed as she had never been kissed before.

The hardness of his mouth buried itself in hers, seeking, demanding, clamouring for a response until she no longer felt herself a separate body, but one with the searing masculine force that threatened to drown her in its fierceness. It was seconds before she realised he had freed her mouth, and she looked up to see him gazing down in to her face with glowing dark eyes.

'I believed you had made a fool of me,' he murmured while his arms held her tightly against him. 'But I was wrong!' Her mouth was possessed once more with the fury of desire, and he breathed the words close to her lips. 'I *wanted* to be wrong, I have never wanted anything more in my life! That is why I came out here to see you, not because Yacub asked me to, but to hear you tell me you did not deceive me!'

'You were wrong,' Lisa assured him huskily. 'If I could have come and told you what was happening I would have, Yusuf; I wanted to.'

She lowered her eyes and looked at the strong brown throat instead of meeting his eyes, but all aspects of him were equally disturbing in the present situation and she felt a shiver slip along her spine as she slid her arms up around his neck, much more certain of herself now that she was more certain of him.

'And I want to believe you, *chérie.*' He brushed the

sun-blonded hair from her brow with his lips and spoke softly. 'I want to be so sure of you that I shall always know what you feel, and never again be in doubt. Is that possible?'

Lifting her face to him, Lisa smiled with a new confidence, her arms around his neck, her hands stroking the black hair at the back of his head. 'It's possible,' she whispered.

'I love you! I love you so much, these past days have tortured me!'

She gazed up at him for a long moment with bright shining eyes, then buried her head against the broadness of his chest. 'Oh, Yusuf, my love!'

He bent his head once more to seek her lips, parting them gently with his before he took her mouth fiercely and hungrily, like a man in desperate need. Her yielding softness moulded to his lean strength, Lisa clung to him, feeling the same desperate hunger in her own body, discovering needs she had not even dreamed of until this moment. Her fingers curled tightly in his thick black hair while her mouth responded willingly to his with an ecstasy she would not have believed herself capable of.

'Will you marry me?' His voice was deep and husky, close to her ear, and Lisa pressed her face to his dark head. 'If your father gives his approval.'

Lifting her head, Lisa looked up at him with glistening blue eyes, a faint teasing smile on her mouth. 'I don't need Daddy's permission to marry you,' she reminded him. 'I love you, and I'm a liberated woman, remember, my darling.'

Yusuf gathered her to him and held her fast, his mouth just above her eager one, warming her lips with his words. 'Not any longer, my love,' he said, and kissed her in such a way that Lisa was of no mind to argue with him.

What readers say about Harlequin Romances

"I can't imagine my reading life without Harlequin."

J.L.,* Sioux Falls, South Dakota

"I get hours of relaxation and enjoyment reading Harlequins."

M.M., Middletown, New York

"I'm really hooked and I love it."

M.S., Richmond, Virginia

"Harlequins help me to escape from housework into a world of romance, adventure and travel."

J.R., Glastonbury, Connecticut

"I have never read a Harlequin that I did not like. They are all wonderful books."

M.H., Hatboro, Pennsylvania